THE END OF THE TALE
And Other Stories

The hare who didn't like being hugged, the spider with a lifetime's work spinning socks for a centipede, the kitten forced to become an unwilling vegetarian, and the monkeys who invented war are just some of the animals who people W. J. Corbett's sparkling collection of sixteen stories. His sharp wit and realistic approach to the nastier sides of human nature give his writing a special zest, and the result is a feast of entertainment for readers young and old alike.

THE END OF
THE TALE

W. J. Corbett

Illustrated by Tony Ross

First published in Great Britain 1985
by
Methuen Children's Books Limited
This Large Print edition published by
Chivers Press
by arrangement with
Methuen Children's Books Limited
and in the U.S.A. with the author
1988

ISBN 0 7451 0723 0

British Library Cataloguing in Publication Data

Corbett, W. J.
   The end of the tale: and other stories.
   —(A Lythway book).
   I. Title   II. Ross, Tony
   823'.914[J]   PZ7

   ISBN 0–7451–0723–0

CONTENTS

BWI

THE END OF THE TALE

THE SPECIAL TREAT

The little centipede was very excited. At last the great day had arrived. He had hardly slept a wink all night thinking about it. Now he was jigging around impatiently as his mother bustled. First she tidied this, then she straightened that, then she remembered something and attended to it before she forgot again. Mothers could be very tiresome, even more so on special days.

The little centipede had been extra good for a whole week. 'A special treat must be earned,' his mother had said. It hadn't been easy. Only yesterday he had been called a goody goody by his best friend. That had hurt a lot. At times he had been tempted to roll in the mud, to shout rude names after his prim and proper aunt, to be just one of the gang again. For it was so boring being good. Lonely too, for all the best games had rules that annoyed the grown-ups. But he was determined to stay on his best behaviour for the special treat was very dear to his heart. So for one whole week he sat alone, counting his legs over and over again for something to do. The only interesting thing about that was the answer.

'How very odd,' said his father, smiling at some secret joke.

'Utter nonsense,' snorted the prim and proper aunt. 'But then, what can we expect when he is always bottom of the class at sums? Ninety-nine legs, indeed. Why it's scandalous. Shocking. Now in my day...'

But of course it wasn't her day. It was the little centipede's special day. And after a whole week of goodness he felt he had earned it.

At last his mother was checking to make sure her bonnet was on straight. That meant she was ready to go. Briskly she set off down the hill, the little centipede scrambling along behind. Soon they reached their destination.

It was a small cave, half-hidden by brambles. At the entrance, smiling and rubbing his hairy legs together, sat the spider-who-span. At least that was how most folk addressed him. The stern aunt back home would have none of that. 'Nonsense,' she would say. 'He is the spider-who-spins.' Others insisted he was the spider-who-spun. The spider himself couldn't have cared less. He made a good living at his trade. Span, spin or spun, he was doing very nicely, thank you.

'And how can we help you this beautiful morning?' he asked, his many eyes glinting as Mother opened her purse.

'Fifty pairs of your finest quality socks if you please,' she replied. 'That will mean one hundred separate items in all, and not'—she frowned at her son—'ninety-nine.'

The little centipede glowed with happiness and pride. None of his friends owned socks. They often scoffed and said socks were posh. But secretly they all yearned for a set. But alas, socks came very expensive, and few families could afford such luxuries in these hard times.

The spider-who-span grinned widely. 'Who's a lucky lad, then?' he said, winking at the little centipede. 'And what colour would he like?'

3

'We thought a sensible plain brown,' began Mother. She then noticed a tear forming in her son's eye. Sighing, she continued, 'Very well, then, as this is a special treat you may choose for yourself.'

'Please, I'd like sky-blue socks with red piping round the tops,' said the little centipede, all in a rush. Shyly he added, 'With garters to keep them up with.'

His mother tut-tutted beneath her breath.

'Bright colours and garters are the fashion these days,' said the spider-who-span. Again he winked encouragingly at the little centipede. Retreating into his cave he soon returned with several skeins of silk, each of a different colour. Sorting through them he quickly found the exact shade the youngster desired. Then he and Mother began to discuss prices and other boring things. All seemed to be going well until Mother raised the question of delivery.

'Fifty days?' she echoed, frowning again. 'Well, we don't know about that. It is a long time to wait. And as you see, my son takes a very small sock size. We

were banking on a day or two at the
latest. Oh dear, this is a problem.'

'I really am very sorry,' shrugged the
spider. 'But the truth is my order book is
chock-a-block full. I'm only taking on
the job as a personal favour. He seems
such a pleasant little chap, and I hate to
disappoint him.' Again he smiled
warmly at the little centipede, winking
with a different eye this time.

'That would work out at one pair a
day, then?' said Mother, doing a quick
bit of reckoning-up.

'Each pair complete with garters,'
pointed out the spider-who-span. 'And
you will find no better quality anywhere.
Still, if you feel you can't wait for real
craftsmanship . . .' He began to gather
up his bundles of silken thread.

'Please, Mother,' begged the little
centipede. 'I don't mind waiting,
honest.'

His mother wavered and fiddled with
the clasp of her purse. 'Well, I really
don't know. But I must admit, your
work is famous for its high quality.'

The spider looked pleased. 'I'll tell
you what,' he said. 'Because I've

developed a liking for our little friend, I'll spin him the first pair right here and now. Plus garters, of course. How's that?'

The little centipede jumped up and down for joy. 'And can I wear them today, Mother? Please say I can.'

Mother looked bewildered. 'Wouldn't it be better to wait until the complete set is ready? Won't it look silly wearing only one pair of socks?'

'With garters,' said the spider quickly. 'And then before you know it there will be another pair, ready and waiting. Why it's almost tomorrow now,' he said, glancing at the sun.

Reluctantly Mother gave in. After paying the spider a small sum in advance, she and the little centipede sat down to wait for the first pair of socks.

The spider-who-span was a wonderful craftsman, there was no doubt about it. His hairy legs fairly flew as he shaped the brightly-coloured silks into the required pattern. In almost no time at all the first pair of socks, plus garters, was finished. Eagerly the little centipede pulled them up his legs, proudly snapping the garters into place with a pleasing 'thwack'.

'Until tomorrow, then?' called the spider, waving them goodbye. 'And if you don't mind my saying, they look very smart indeed. Have a good day.'

Back home the little centipede was the envy of all his friends. They didn't jeer at all when he explained that the rest of the set would be coming along later. They were fascinated by the garters, each taking turns to have a snap. He even let his best friend try them on. All agreed that one pair of socks was better than no socks at all.

Each day the little centipede returned to the cave of the spider-who-span. Home once more, he had yet another pair of socks to be admired by all and sundry. And he played rough games with his friends, happy that he no longer needed to be good any more. Soon the fiftieth day came around.

He was just about to set off for the cave when his aunt noticed something. 'Good gracious, if he hasn't worn his first pair of socks clean through,' she said, in a shocked voice. 'Didn't I say socks should be kept for Sunday wear

only? Didn't your mother suggest that you wait until the full set was completed? Now, thanks to disobedience, this has happened.'

And it had. The first pair of socks had great holes in the toes and heels. Mother inspected them closely. Then her eyes wandered to the second pair. They too were beginning to look rather frayed.

'Heavens above,' she wailed. 'This is what comes of pandering to the wishes of the young. I should have known this would happen.' And she gave the little centipede a good hiding.

The next morning she didn't even check to see if her bonnet was on straight. Grimly she marched down to the cave, the shame-faced little centipede scrambling along behind. The spider-who-span spied them coming.

'It will be the rough and tumble,' he said sympathetically. 'After all, the best of socks wear out eventually. But what a pity, eh? Oh well, here is the last pair of the order, plus garters.'

Tearfully, the little centipede pulled on his last pair of new socks. He was much too upset to snap the garters this

9

time.

'Is there any advice you could give us?' implored Mother. 'We know it isn't your fault. We are not complaining about the quality. If the truth is known, it's my son's own fault. He would insist upon wearing them every day. His friends too, for they were always trying them on, and snapping at the garters.'

'That's the trouble with the young,' agreed the spider-who-span, shaking his head. 'They think every day is Sunday. They are never content to wait for a full set of anything. I have encountered this problem many times before. Ideally, socks should all wear out together, at the same time. I'm afraid we have here what we call in the trade, a never-ending worry.'

'And just look at that second pair,' wept Mother. 'They are almost as frayed as the first. They will be hanging off his feet by tomorrow. He thinks money grows on trees. After all my scrimping and saving, just look at the state of those socks.'

'Actually, I'm a bit concerned about that third pair,' said the spider, peering

10

closely at his handiwork. 'They appear to be splitting at the seams, unless my eyes deceive me.'

'Heaven preserve us,' sobbed Mother. 'Brand new socks at the back, and raggeddy old things at the front. Well, there's nothing else for it. We will have to order three new pairs, though where the money is coming from . . .'

The spider-who-span looked embarrassed. 'I hate to remind you, but I did mention what we call in the trade, an on-going worry. I can certainly spin you three more pairs of socks over the next three days, but just glance at that fourth pair. They are beginning to look rather ropy, don't you think? I'm afraid the problem is travelling all down his legs, poor little chap.'

Mother mopped at her eyes with a large red hankie. 'There's no hope at all, then?' she whispered.

'There is only one thing to be done, but I warn you it's drastic,' said the spider, solemnly. 'A complete, whole new set of socks, to be worn all together, and only on Sundays. In other words, to start afresh. That is the only way to stop

11

the rot.'

'With garters?' asked the little centipede, brightening.

'One must keep up with the trends of fashion,' replied the spider, looking grave, but flashing yet another wink at the little centipede. His eyes gleamed as Mother counted the money in her purse.

'We can't really afford it, but if we must, we must,' she replied, heavy-heartedly. 'When can we expect them to be ready?'

The little centipede whooped for joy, and began tugging off his old socks. 'Please could I have green ones with purple stripes this time?' he begged.

The grown-ups ignored him. 'Ah, yes, the completion date,' said the spider slowly. 'A slight problem there. As you know, my order-book is chock-a-block full at the moment. But I'll tell you what. How about if I spin him a pair right now, to be going on with? Then, working on a pair a day ... will fifty days be all right?'

A change came over Mother. Firmly she snapped her purse closed. 'I have a much better idea of my own,' she said angrily. 'He can learn to do without socks. He managed before, he can do so again. This is the last special treat he will get out of me. Look at him all bare-legged, and aching to pull yet another first pair on. And his friends, as soon as we get home. Not likely, I'm not going through that again.'

'How about a nice warm scarf?' suggested the spider-who-span. 'Or a balaclava hat? Half-price for a good customer. Hey—'

But Mother was already half-way down the hill, the little centipede snivelling and scrambling along behind.

Sadly, the spider began to pack his skeins of silk away. Just then he heard a voice. Turning, he saw another lady centipede. Beside her giggled two girl centipedes. The spider's eyes widened as Mother began to fiddle with the clasp of her purse. With a broad smile he advanced, tape-measure at the ready.

'Good morning, lovely ladies,' he said, winking slyly at the smaller ones. 'Could I guess and say we are here to discuss a special treat?'

The mother looked surprised. 'As a

matter of fact, yes. For my twin daughters. We were thinking about house-slippers...'

'And charming they'll look,' said the beaming spider.

'I will pay a small sum in advance, of course,' said Mother, counting out coins. 'So when do you think they could be ready?'

The spider was suddenly solemn. 'You will appreciate I am highly regarded in the trade,' he said. 'And as a result my order-book is always chock-a-block full. But for such pretty girls I will make a special offer. I will spin the first pair right here and now, and the rest over a period of one hundred days. How will that suit you?'

'You mean one pair each, immediately?' asked the confused lady, spilling coins upon the ground as she tried to reckon up. 'And, did I hear you right, the rest spread out until Kingdom Come?'

'I had in mind an immediate pair between them,' the spider replied, his eyes dulling as the coins were returned to the purse. He became persuasive. 'I

14

could spin them in an hour or two. And see, it's almost tomorrow now,' he glanced hopefully at the sun.

'Well, I really don't know,' said Mother. 'We thought a day or two at the most. My twins take a very small slipper size.'

'And please, we would like yellow slippers, with blue stars on them,' begged the pair.

'And why not? Blue stars are all the rage these days,' said the spider-who-span, winking cheekily again. Now *his* eyes were like stars as Mother began to fumble through the clinking money in her purse. But she still seemed a little hesitant.

'It seems an awfully long time to wait for a mere hundred pairs of house-slippers,' she remarked, shaking her head.

'With pom-poms,' chorused the giggling girls.

'Indeed. What are house-slippers without pom-poms?' smiled the spider who span, spinned and spun. Eagerly he clutched at Mother's coins, tucking them carefully away. He was soon hard at work, his nimble legs a blur of speed. Though she could only admire his skill, Mother looked worried nevertheless. Not so the girls. They had been good for a whole week. It hadn't been easy. They now believed they had earned their special treat. They jigged impatiently, hardly able to wait to try on their first house-slipper each ... plus pom-pom. The future looked sweet indeed. But for Mother sitting quietly and thinking, the future appeared a little less rosy. She could sense 'an on-going worry' beginning to loom. So could the spider-who-span, for his smile was much too wide for comfort...

BAN THE MUSHROOM

He was named Bartholemew. For a glossy black kitten with sea-green eyes the choice was perfect.

He was an obedient little cat. Often, while having a quiet snooze, his mistress would wake him to enquire why he wasn't playing with his ball of wool, or scrambling in and out of her house-slippers? This could be annoying. But Bartholemew wouldn't have hurt his mistress for the world. He would yawn and stretch, perhaps half-heartedly chase his tail, before slumping back into his basket. Snoozing, that's what Bartholemew liked best. Mealtimes too. He loved mealtimes.

His mouth always watered when his mistress took the tin-opener from its hook in the kitchen. Would it be those delicious little fishes, packed in their flat tin, and swimming in oil? Or maybe those savoury chunks he was so fond of? It was nice to wonder about such things as he waited for his special bowl to be pushed beneath his nose. These were times he could forgive her for the itchy blue ribbon he was forced to wear about his neck. All in all, life was sweet for a green-eyed cat called Bartholemew.

He believed he knew his mistress well. But he didn't. After all, he was only three months old. Only slowly was he beginning to learn that mistresses were subject to strange moods. His mistress in particular.

She was a lonely lady. She had neat grey hair, and wore spectacles to peer at the labels on cat-food tins. She watched television a lot, especially in the evenings. Her favourite programmes were 'Crossroads', and wildlife films. She often said to the odd person she met that it was Bartholemew who was the 'Crossroads' fan. She maintained that he followed the plot closely. This was not true. Bartholemew thought 'Crossroads' was tripe. He liked cat-food adverts best of all. But it was a wildlife film they watched together one evening that brought about the strange change in his mistress. Bartholemew was licking the last scrap of sardine from his bowl when

18

things began to go badly wrong.

Immediately the film was over she jumped angrily from her chair, and began to rummage about in her big cupboard. She was searching for a large piece of cardboard. Finding it, she took a stick of bright red chalk, and to Bartholemew's great surprise, drew a neat picture of his supper on it. Then, underneath her sketch she scrawled some words:

Protect the Whale
from extinction

Though Bartholemew couldn't read, the grim look on her face told him to keep his head down. From that time onwards, life became very unfair for a once-contented cat.

The next morning they were up early. Apparently they had lots of things to do that day. After an unusual breakfast of milky gruel, revolting stuff for a cat brought up on whales, Bartholemew sat and watched his mistress tack the piece of cardboard onto a broom-handle, and put her hat and coat on. A few minutes later they were outside Mr Brown's the grocer, protesting for all they were worth about the whales in his cat-food tins. According to his mistress, Bartholemew took a very dim view of it all, which wasn't true. Stung to anger, Mr Brown said he was merely trying to make an honest penny, and the only whale he knew about was the one in the film *Moby Dick*. Who did Bartholemew think he was, he fumed. He had never complained before. In fact Bartholemew wasn't complaining, his mistress was, and he was getting the blame for it. And so began a distressing period in Bartholemew's life. Once he had looked forward to mealtimes, now he loathed them. For Bartholemew, much against his will, became a vegetarian. Morning, noon and night he was fed mushrooms in milk. Sometimes his mistress slipped him the odd nut cutlet to vary his diet, but even they became rarer. For the fields at the back of their cottage abounded with nourishing mushrooms. Soon the delicious taste of tinned whales in oil became a memory. At last Bartholemew's patience snapped.

One night he slunk out of the cottage, vowing never to return. His own cat at last, he roamed the village streets. It was in a dustbin that he came upon the familiar can, a sight he had once believed he would never see again. And, gloriously, there was one small whale still left inside, swimming in oil. Bartholemew hungrily bolted it down. He felt no guilt at all. For surely anything that could taste so delicious had no right to be protected? It was then he made another vow. Never again would a mushroom ever insult his palate. For if the whales wouldn't come to him, he would go to the whales. In short, he would become a scavenger, and the village dustbins would provide the food he loved so much. But the competition soon proved fierce, for like most villages, this one had more than its quota of ravenous moggies. Soon Bartholemew's glossy black fur became dull and bedraggled. His eyes, still sea-green but these days usually half-closed from constant battle, became wary and cunning. His body ached from the kicks of Mr Brown the grocer, who liked to lurk just inside his shop doorway, hoping to catch Bartholemew slinking by. But never once did Bartholemew consider returning home. For much as he missed his comfort, the thought of those loathsome mushrooms turned his stomach. He just could not face that fare again.

Sometimes he saw his ex-mistress in the village High Street. As usual she was banning something or other. It could be anything—the banning of hooks from fishing lines, or protesting against the theft of silk from silkworms. But despite all her activities, she never ceased to mourn the loss of her green-eyed pet. Most nights would find her settling down to watch 'Crossroads' with tears in her eyes.

Winter came and Bartholemew, curled up in a cold alley-way, would think longingly of his warm basket by that cheerful fireside. He found it comforting to dream about the good old days before all the whale banning nonsense. In his mind's eye he liked to

23

picture the hand of his ex-mistress reaching to take the tin-opener from its hook, and the can with its free-offer label coming down from the top shelf. Amazingly, Bartholemew even missed good old 'Crossroads'. The skipping paper-lad seemed to be forever whistling its catchy tune. And wasn't Christmas just around the corner? Soon the tall glittering tree would be going up in the Motel Reception, hung with tinsel and chocolate mice. But always the image of stewed mushrooms intruded, and Bartholemew would steel his heart against ever returning home.

Then, one bitter day in January, Bartholemew once again saw his old mistress in the High Street. He was not surprised to see a banner in her hand. Curious, Bartholemew nipped across the street to take a closer look. What he saw made his heart jump for joy. Sketched in red chalk on her latest cardboard sign was a huge mushroom. Beneath it, scrawled in a shaky hand were the words

BAN THE BOMB

Words, of course, meant nothing to Bartholemew. But the picture did. At last she had seen sense. She had finally realised how cruelly she had treated her pet, and was trying to make amends. Well, Bartholemew was a forgiving cat. And all things considered, January was the ideal month for him to come in from the cold. Without more ado a delighted Bartholemew turned and streaked off for home. He didn't stay to see his mistress cease her marching up and down. Ignoring Mr Brown, she insultingly entered the Fish and Veg store next door. Emerging with her purchases she set off for home, basket on one hand, banner in the other. Of course, Bartholemew had beaten her to it. To her surprise and delight he was waiting on the front doorstep. Tearfully she invited him in, fussing and worrying about the state of his matted fur and battered eyes. Then it was time for tea and 'Crossroads'.

Contentedly, Bartholemew curled up in his basket by the fire. To pass the time until tea he idly beat time to the 'Crossroads' tune with the tip of his tail.

Oh, but it was bliss to be warm for the first time in many weeks! And to make his happiness complete his mistress was at this very moment in the kitchen, preparing a meal fit for a real cat. Smugly, he listened for the tin-opener coming down from its hook. So what would it consist of, this spread? Succulent, unbanned, canned whales, swimming in oil? Or perhaps those meaty chunks he loved so much? Either would tickle a jaded cat's taste-buds. And of course a bowl of cream to follow . . .

His mistress, overjoyed to have him back, was indeed preparing a banquet. From her basket she took a bag of mixed nuts for the cutlets she planned, and, humming happily, popped the mushrooms, freshly picked from the field at the bottom of the garden, into a saucepan of simmering oatmeal gruel. It was just like old times with Bartholemew home, she thought. She expected that at this moment he was catching up with the 'Crossroads' confusing story-line. And there was a good wildlife film on telly later. Which reminded her. Did those callous people down under really stuff kangaroos into cat-food tins? That evening, she thought grimly, she and Bartholemew would sit down and write a really sharp letter to the Australian Government. It was too much. First the poor whales and now kangaroos. Bartholemew would certainly protest against such an outrage. First thing in the morning Mr Brown would find them outside his shop with their banner . . .

Bartholemew didn't wait for the morning. That evening he took one sniff at his tea, leapt from his basket, and disappeared for ever.

ALL'S FAIR IN LOVE
AND WAR

Once each week the two friends met beneath the old fig tree. After exchanging warm greetings they would set about gathering up the fallen figs into a neat pile. This usually took some time for they liked to pause and chat as friends are wont to do. But this particular morning their conversation was strained. This was because the Blue Monkey had entered the clearing carrying a length of finely-crafted wood. It had a firm paw grip, and a wicked knobbly end. The Red Monkey, ever the nervous type, pondered long and hard as his friend laid it carefully down at the edge of the clearing. Just as the Red Monkey was about to question his friend about this puzzling object, the Blue Monkey, cheerful as always, glanced at the sky and spoke.

'Best get the figs gathered up quickly,' he remarked. 'For it looks like rain. And I'd hate you to catch cold on the way home.'

'Why should I catch cold on the way home?' asked the Red Monkey, suspiciously. 'If I should catch cold, why shouldn't you?'

But the Blue Monkey was already gathering together the fallen figs. As he busied himself he made a very strange remark indeed. He said that having to share the figs this way hardly filled the stomachs of his family.

Those throw-away words, plus the added worry of the unexplained length of wood at the edge of the clearing, set the Red Monkey to more anxious pondering. Surely, he thought, his friend didn't begrudge him his fair portion of figs? No, it was impossible. Close friends never thought such things. But his mounting suspicion caused him to be extra careful about the dividing up of the figs that morning. He made sure to check his own hoard twice, as well as counting and re-counting the pile of his friend, much to that one's amusement. Then it started to rain.

'Never rains but it pours,' remarked the Blue Monkey, cheerfully. 'Best gather up your figs for I'd hate you to catch a chill...'

By now the Red Monkey was worried out of his mind and began to do just that. He had barely gathered his share of the figs to his chest when he felt a heavy blow upon his head. The figs flew from his paws as he slumped to the ground, hazily watching stars float before his eyes. Glancing up he saw through a mist of pain the Blue Monkey hefting his carved piece of wood, and looking triumphant. He was also speaking excitedly.

'Up for three nights I was,' he said. 'Carving and designing. Would it work ... wouldn't it work? I decided to call my new invention a club. And isn't it effective? Thanks to my brilliant invention I shall be returning home with twice as many figs as usual. Frankly, I don't know how I've managed without a club for so long. So goodbye, old friend, and hurry home out of the rain. I wouldn't wish you to go down with something nasty...'

With that he scooped up both portions of figs, and, tucking his

marvellous invention under his arm, set off for home.

It was a confused Red Monkey who staggered to his feet, and unsteadily made his own way homewards. He was empty-pawed and still reeling from the unexpected blow, yet he could not help feeling a sneaking admiration for his friend. Arriving, he was confronted by his hungry family. He explained what had happened, and they angrily scoffed, calling him all sorts of a fool for falling for such a trick.

Before he fell asleep that night the Red Monkey vowed to get even with his friend the Blue Monkey. The next morning, snuffling and sniffing, for he was full of cold, he sat down to invent something even more effective than a club. His yearning for vengeance came to his aid. Within four days he had cracked the problem. Three days later he set off to meet his friend beneath the fig tree, filled with a confidence he had never known before.

The Blue Monkey was already there and waiting. He looked confident too, as he stood whirling his club at the edge of the clearing. But when he saw the strange object in the paw of the Red Monkey, he seemed to pale a little. Now it was his turn to feel nervous. Whatever could it be, he wondered? Puzzled, he put down his club, noting with unease the jaunty way his friend likewise set down his burden. His worry increased as his companion spoke.

'In for a heatwave, I wouldn't doubt,' said the Red Monkey, cheerfully, and glancing at the shimmering blue sky. 'Best get the figs gathered, eh? Wouldn't want you to get sunstroke, old pal.'

'Why should I get sunstroke?' said the suspicious Blue Monkey. 'If I get it, why shouldn't you?'

But the Red Monkey was already gathering together the fallen figs. As he busied himself he made a very strange remark indeed. He said that sharing figs had never been much of an idea, and that thanks to his friend's club he had learned a lot these past few days. That morning, never had two monkeys been more cautious as they divided one pile of figs into two portions. Indeed, neither bothered to check his own pile, each being more concerned about the quantity of his partner's. But, deep down, both monkeys knew that all this checking and re-checking was now a farce. Only one of them would walk away with his paws full of figs that day. Then the sun broke from behind a patchy cloud and glared down.

'Heat I've known, but this ... whew ...' remarked the Red Monkey. 'Best gather up your figs, old friend, for the sun on the back of your neck and all ...'

Hastily the Blue Monkey dashed to pick up his club. He had barely grasped its comforting paw grip before he felt a tremendous blow beneath his ear. He sank to the ground to count stars. Glancing up he saw as if in a dream the Red Monkey picking up from the ground a large, smooth rock.

'It worked!' he was shouting excitedly, hefting it. 'Don't you agree that my new invention makes clubs a thing of the past? I call it a missile ... a guided missile. It's the modern way of obtaining other folks' figs. No offence old friend, and watch that hot sun on the back of your neck as you stagger home . . .'

With that he swept up both piles of fruit and, tucking his amazing missile under his arm, hurried for home.

It was a good hour before the Blue Monkey felt well enough to get to his feet. Bemused, he made his way back home. His family greeted him shrilly. Where were the figs, they demanded. He was in no mood to argue for he felt too feverish and ill. He tottered off to bed with a severe case of sunstroke.

As he recovered, so the Blue Monkey thought long and hard. Soon the day came around when he was due to meet his friend beneath the fig tree. He set off extra early, filled with confidence, for his inventive mind had figured out a plan. Significantly, he left his club at home.

'You're early,' said the Red Monkey, suspiciously. He entered the clearing, carefully setting down his missile within easy reach. Then he glanced around, his mind working furiously as he failed to spot what he sought. He spoke again, nervously. 'So where's your club this morning?'

'Come and sit down, old pal,' said the Blue Monkey, cheerfully. 'Let's get this sorry state of affairs thrashed out. I've left my club at home as a gesture of goodwill, for I dearly wish to bury the hatchet.'

'What's a hatchet?' said the Red Monkey, quickly. Again he peered around the clearing.

'Nothing to get alarmed about,' soothed the other. 'Just a small invention I was working on, but I haven't brought it along, honest. For I wish only for us to be sharing friends again. How long have we known one another?'

'It's true we've lived in peace all our lives,' replied the Red Monkey, relaxing and sitting down. 'But don't forget it was you who brought about this state of un-peace with that club of yours...'

The Blue Monkey grimaced. 'Un-peace,' he echoed. 'Such a clumsy word for the exciting new skill I invented ... But that's all behind us, I hope.'

'So do I,' said the Red Monkey. Then he looked wistful. 'But you are right, it was exciting. Especially when my

36

missile hit you smack on the head, and I ran off home with all the figs. But I too am prepared to put this un-peace behind us and share the bounty of the fig tree, as we used to.'

The Blue Monkey frowned. 'That word "un-peace",' he said. 'If it weren't for the fact that we have agreed to put that behind us, I would be inclined to invent a shorter, sharper word for such an exciting pastime. But never mind, come, let us gather the figs up, and share them equally. And quickly, for I smell a storm on the way, and I'd hate you to be struck by lightning . . .'

'Why should I be struck by lightning?' began the Red Monkey, all suspicious again. But his friend was already gathering up the figs. Soon they were working side by side, chatting together as they used to do. Despite the black clouds gathering above, the scene beneath the fig tree was one of peace and comradeship. And then came the dividing up of the spoils.

'Now gather your share up, and I'll see you next week,' said the Blue Monkey, patting his friend on the back in a reassuring manner.

The Red Monkey, feeling a great warmth for the other, nodded and smiled as he picked up his figs. His missile he ignored, for he surely had no need for it any more. He made to leave the clearing along his old familiar path, but was brought to a halt by the voice of his friend.

'Why not take the short cut?' said the Blue Monkey. 'For if I'm not mistaken that storm will break any moment, and remember about the lightning . . .'

'Well, I know my old route is longer,' said the Red Monkey, shyly. 'But it's prettier, you see. I like to enjoy the view as I stroll home. But perhaps you are right, what with the storm coming on. I will take the short cut today. And thank you for worrying about my welfare, old friend.'

'Think nothing of it,' replied the Blue Monkey, smoothly. He watched narrow-eyed as the other strode confidently off along the short cut. Suddenly there came the sound of breaking twigs, followed by a loud yell of shock and pain. Whooping triumphantly, the Blue Monkey raced along the short cut path, and peered into the hole he had dug, and cunningly covered with twigs and grass, early that morning. At the bottom slumped his bruised and bewildered friend. All around the hole lay his figs, which had flown from his paws as he had sought to save himself. The gleeful Blue Monkey began to gather them up.

'What do you think of my Red Monkey trap?' he called down the hole. 'It took a lot of working out, I'll tell you. I had to figure out the correct depth and width, and to make sure that the grass on top was fresh, so you wouldn't cotton on . . .'

'You swore we were finished with the un-peace,' bawled the Red Monkey, struggling as he tried to clamber up the smooth side of the hole.

'And so we have,' replied the Blue Monkey, pleasantly. 'For I never liked that clumsy word. I have decided to re-name our exciting new pastime. You and I are making history, my friend, for between us we have invented War.'

'War!' cried the other. 'What about all

the peace and the sharing, and living together as brothers?'

'What indeed?' replied the thoughtful Blue Monkey, his mind's-eye for one brief moment glimpsing the future. But he was soon his cheerful self again. Gathering up both portions of figs he returned home to prepare for the next round that he knew was bound to follow.

'Mind you,' he mused to himself. 'Inventing war just to gain a few extra figs does seem a waste. What my friend and I want is something worthwhile to go to war over. I think I'll tell him and his family to shove off out of this wood before he tells me to. And if they refuse ... well, I'll soon invent something to change their minds. After all, all's fair in love and war as my friend will agree...'

TUMF

For six days of the week Tumf was an ordinary young elephant. On those days he lived inside a circle of aunts and was pampered and spoiled, for they loved him dearly.

'Only the ripest bananas for Tumf,' they would say. 'And the plumpest, for he wishes to grow big and strong like his father.'

Sometimes his mother would squeeze into the circle for a glimpse of her son. Anxiously she would say, 'I hope Tumf isn't being ruined with all this attention.'

Gently she would be squeezed out again. 'We know what is best for Tumf,' the aunts would reply. 'Another hand of bananas for our precious.'

Tumf endured all the fuss. When he was quite full he would settle down to play with his drum. The hollow log provided by the aunts made a delightful sound when tapped smartly with the tip of his trunk. 'Tumf' it would go. And, more tunefully, 'Tumf ti tumf tumf', for he was skilled at making up tunes. And his aunts would sway with enjoyment for they loved both him and his music. And so for those six days of the week he lived his life deep in the jungle, deep inside the circle of adoring aunts. All except for Tuesdays.

Tuesdays were special. They were Tumf's days for pretending and dreaming. Each Tuesday morning he would wander off alone and become something else until the sun went down. Last Tuesday he had imagined himself a beautiful white bird with a yellow beak. All that day he had soared and hovered over the tree-tops, feeling as light and as free as thistledown. But his day had been a little spoiled. For if there was one thing Tumf hated it was for someone to play his drum without his permission.

'Tumf tumf tumf' the sound of his drum came floating out of the jungle. It was his aunts calling him home, for the sun was going down. Reluctantly he had obeyed the call.

'And what were we today?' they asked, plying him with bananas. 'A beautiful white bird with a yellow beak? Well, we never. And did you miss us dreadfully?'

'Tumf tumf tumf' the annoyed young elephant shook his head as he tapped out tunes on his drum.

Soon Tuesday came around again. 'Today I shall be a little black ant,' he said to himself. So saying, he set off for the Plain where the ants built castles in the sun. Whilst marching along behind the soldier ants he had a visitor.

'And what have we here?' asked the green spider with glittering eyes. Just passing, his curiosity had been aroused by Tumf's strange behaviour.

'I'm a little black ant,' explained the young elephant. 'It's Tuesday, you see.'

'I never doubted it,' replied the green spider, squatting comfortably upon his many hairy legs. 'It so happens Tuesday is my special day too. Especially Tuesday tea-time. For guess what I always fancy for tea on Tuesdays?'

Tumf said he was much too busy to play guessing games. A little black ant's work was never done, he declared.

The green spider watched with

amusement as Tumf crawled about amongst the castles. For their part the real ants thought him a thorough nuisance, but kept their distance for fear of being rolled on.

'Well, I'll tell you,' said the spider, with a grin. 'There is nothing quite so tasty as little black ants for Tuesday tea-time. What do you think about that? Are you terribly afraid?'

Tumf certainly was. Now he was wishing he was a young elephant again, safe in the jungle, safe in the circle of his aunts. He fearfully watched as the green spider, still broadly smiling, rose to his toes and advanced. With a loud trumpet Tumf scrambled up and began to lumber away as fast as he could go.

'Lovely grub,' yelled the spider, entering into the spirit of things. He hadn't had so much fun in ages. He set off in pursuit.

Tumf, still living out his fantasy, was now a badly frightened little black ant. His blind dash across the Plain soon led him to the brink of disaster. Only just in time did he manage to check his flight, as suddenly before him yawned the

Bottomless Gorge, waiting to swallow another victim. For one awful moment Tumf teetered on the edge. Wildly glancing behind he saw the green spider, eyes glittering, jaws ravening for tea. Then suddenly a slender ray of hope was offered to a little black ant. For across the gorge from lip to lip trembled a single strand of spider web, shimmering in the setting sun. Delicate and fine, it could not possibly be swarmed by a fat green spider with glittering eyes. But a little black ant ... Tumf leaned forward, his foot reaching out to tread that path to salvation. No longer was the spider grinning. On his face was now a look of horror, for what had begun as a joke seemed about to end in a death. Then suddenly it was dusk, and ...

'Tumf, tumf, tumf' across the Plain came the sound of his drum calling him home. Abruptly Tumf drew back from the void. Turning, he lumbered off, feeling extremely annoyed. He did so wish his aunts wouldn't play his drum without permission. He also felt angry about the fat green spider with glittering eyes. Tumf hated to have his daydreams interrupted by strangers. He decided that next Tuesday he would pretend to be an extra-large black spider with evil eyes who enjoyed green spiders for tea. That would teach a certain someone a lesson. Some time later an exceedingly lucky young elephant arrived safely home.

The moon rode high, as deep in the jungle a circle was filled, and the tropical air vibrated with the sound of a solemnly rhythmic, 'tumf ti tumf tumf . . . tumf ti tumf tumf' of a drum . . .

A HUG FOR JASON

Jason Harebell lived with his widowed mother in a hole at the edge of the wood. An only child, he was hugged a lot when he wasn't expecting it. He hated that. But then, all young hares dislike being hugged. It was just his luck that the wood was filled with wolves who loved to hug hares. Given a choice, Jason would have avoided the wood like the plague. His mother, however, had other ideas. She spent much of her life writing notes to Grandma on crisp white paper. She always had a big pile of notes in her writing-desk drawer. For, not content with scribbling down the day's happenings, she liked to write about tomorrow too, for she was clever at looking into the future.

The month being June, already July's notes were neatly stacked, and waiting for their date of delivery, each addressed to Grandma Harebell. Unfortunately, Grandma lived on the other side of the wood in a hole quite similar to Jason's, but roomier, for she had a weight problem. Gloomily, Jason eyed the note his mother was holding out to him.

'I'd deliver it myself,' she said. 'But I have one of my splitting headaches. And as you know, the closeness of the trees in the wood always makes my headaches worse.'

Jason wasn't fooled for one moment. His mother never ever delivered her own notes for a good reason: because it would involve a risky journey through the wood. It was extremely selfish of her, for Jason hated that part of the world himself. He suspected she didn't much care for him, despite all the hugging.

'Don't be such a silly lad,' she chided, when he protested yet again. 'The wolves will be fast asleep, as like as not. Just remember to walk on tip-toe as your late daddy did before he got hugged by a wolf. And don't lose that note, it's very important. Off you go, now.'

She gave him a quick hug before taking up her pen again. It seemed she had forgotten his existence as she closed her eyes and pondered about autumn loneliness, and how it felt to be all on one's own, with only a crisp writing-pad for comfort.

Reluctantly, Jason set off through the wood. He was quite fond of his mother but he did wish she wouldn't tell so many lies. She always insisted that the wolves in the wood would be fast asleep. This was nonsense. Wolves were early risers, and were up and about hugging everything in sight, long before the sun rose. And as for walking on tip-toe, a fat lot of good that would do. It was whilst delivering one of mother's notes on tip-toe that his father had met his end. Sometimes Jason believed that his mother only needed him for a messenger, though she did seem fond of him in her absent-minded way. And she hugged him often, even if Jason did hate it. But, he would often think, if his mother really loved him, she would stop writing all those notes to Grandma Harebell. Then he wouldn't have to keep risking his life in the wood. But it was a forlorn hope. Mother was too set in her ways to change now.

Jason was lucky that day. Not one wolf did he see. But he was in no mood to wonder where they had all got to. He was simply thankful to be emerging from the trees, glad to catch that first glimpse of Grandma's vegetable patch.

'Eh?' shrilled Grandma Harebell. She was very hard of hearing. 'A note, you say? What note, I've got no note? Only reply to them, myself. Never write them much. Never found the time, what with all my lettuces and cabbages springing up for picking.'

'It's a note from Mother!' shouted Jason. He handed her the crisply folded paper.

'What, another?' grumbled Grandma. She snatched, and read it aloud:

Dear Mama;

You will notice that the bearer of this note is a complete stranger. You will be sad to learn that I had to find another messenger after our Jason was hugged by a wolf in the wood. Oh, I am upset. I would come and see you, but I've got one of my splitting headaches. Must

51

close for now, for I have a lot of notes to write.

Lots of love

P.S. Sorry, I meant bunions.

'Stuff and nonsense,' snorted Grandma Harebell. She peered at Jason. 'Stranger? You look the same as always to me. And if she meant bunions, she should have said so in the first place. She always has to write a P.S.'

'She did say bunions,' Jason pointed out.

'Well, in my opinion this note is rubbish,' said Grandma. 'And I intend to reply and tell her so. I'm only replying, mind, for I never write notes much.'

Jason sat down beside the vegetable patch while Grandma penned a stinging reply. He was completely bewildered. He felt so very much alive. So why should his mother write that he had been hugged by a wolf in the wood? He couldn't understand it at all.

'That's that, then,' said Grandma,

signing her reply with a flourish. She gave it to him, the while peering into his face. 'Now, hold that reply tightly,' she said. 'And don't forget to tip-toe through the wood, for all the good it will do. Image of your late father, you are. But at least the mystery is solved. Hugged by a wolf, indeed. Any fool can see that this note is dated Friday the thirteenth of June . . .'

'And today is Thursday the twelfth of June,' said Jason, counting in his head.

'She's got her dates mixed up somewhere,' snorted Grandma. 'And now be off with you, I have to water my prize onions.'

Jason set off for home. He had one narrow escape. A lone wolf slipped from behind a tree and tried to give him a quick hug. Jason had long known that tip-toeing was pointless. He took to his heels and never once stopped until he had reached the safety of the other side of the wood.

Mother read Grandma's reply carefully. Then she read it again. For a while she was as puzzled as her son.

'How very odd,' she frowned. 'Mama

says you are not a bit like a stranger, but the same young nuisance who always delivers my notes. And she says, if I mean bunions I should say so. Didn't I say so?'

'You did,' said Jason. 'But Grandma thinks you have got your dates mixed up.'

Absently, Mrs Harebell hugged her son as she studied the date on the note. Then she smiled and shook her head. 'Of course. How silly of me. I gave you the wrong note. This note was meant to be delivered tomorrow, Friday the thirteenth of June. Fancy me making a mistake like that. Never mind, you can deliver the real today's note tomorrow. Better late than never, eh?'

She reached into her drawer and drew out a crisp white note from the pile. Jason wanted to discuss the worrying question of his supposed death in the wood, but she shushed him soothingly. She said she had a splitting headache, and felt much too unwell to listen to the prattle of foolish children. So saying, she hugged him good-night, and retired to bed.

Jason rose early the next morning. The truth was, he had slept little the previous night. For the thought of another trip through the wood appalled him. His mother brushed aside his protests. As usual she had another of her splitting headaches.

'You know I'd go myself,' she said, wincing with pain. 'Off you go, and don't forget to tip-toe. Explain to Grandma about the note mix-up. So what are you dawdling for?'

Clutching yesterday's note, Jason hurried off through the wood. Sadly, he was out of luck that Friday the thirteenth of June. He was quickly hugged by a wolf in the dead centre of the wood. The crisp white note fluttered to the ground. It read:

Dear Mama,

I am writing to tell you about an awful dream I had. I dreamt that our little Jason suffered the same fate as his father whilst tip-toeing through the wood. Please

56

reply for I am very worried, and I have a splitting headache.

Lots of love

P.S. How are your onions?

But Grandma never wrote notes. She only ever replied to them. And she could hardly reply to a note she had not received in the first place...

THE NUT COMMITTEE

The sudden change in the weather should not have been surprising here in England. Winter still, yet for one week the sun had shone warm, the winds falling to feather-soft. Now, this morning, the sky was overcast and filled with flurries of snow, and a returned east wind whipped through the bare branches of the trees. The season had regained its grip. That false spring would mean hardship for some who lived in the Arden Woods.

Shivering, his fur white with snow, Redd Squirrel crouched outside the hollow tree. He knew that he was being kept waiting deliberately. At least an hour ago a head had poked outside, to quickly vanish. Then followed much whispering and laughter from within. At long last the occupants seemed to tire of their petty game. A sharp voice bid Redd enter. Stiff with cold, but stern with pride, he did.

The warmth inside the hollow tree set

Redd's chilblains throbbing, but he bravely bore the pain. He was out of the biting wind and for that he was thankful. As he thawed out, Redd warily eyed the Nut Committee. Three in number, they were fat and each a dingy shade of grey. They returned his gaze through mean eyes, as if savouring this moment. For at last, standing humbly before them was the famed Redd Squirrel, come down in the world and reduced to begging. Behind the trio was the source of their power. Stacked and carefully counted was a hoard of succulent nuts, purposely displayed so as to cause eyes to glisten and mouths to water.

'State your full name,' snapped the Chairman, both the fattest around the middle and sitting in the middle.

'The Honourable Redd of Ardenwood,' came the reply.

'Why so modest?' sneered the Vice-Chairman. 'Don't you red squirrels usually have fancy family mottoes?'

'If you must know, my family motto is *Help the Needy*,' replied Redd, controlling his temper.

'That will look posh in red ink,'

taunted the Secretary. He sat on the right, his left-pawed pen poised over a thick ledger. Soon Redd's full name and family motto were entered into the book in beautiful copper-plate writing. After carefully blotting his work, the Secretary looked up at Redd, his eyes narrow.

'Help the needy, and he can't even help himself,' smirked the Chairman. His expression hardened. 'I suppose you know that any nuts you borrow will have to be repaid many times over when the autumn comes? But don't let's waste time. State your case, for no doubt there is a long queue outside, waiting their turn.'

'Actually, there isn't,' said Redd. 'In fact, I am your only customer this morning.'

The Nut Committee glanced at each other in astonishment. They had been hoping that the false spring had caught many fools out. Could it be that the poor squirrels of Arden Wood were learning to save a few nuts, instead of scoffing them all at the merest glimpse of sun? Or were they afraid to come borrowing on account that they were already up to their eyeballs in debt to the Committee? Whatever the reason for their absence, it was worrying. For the Nut Committee had grown enormously rich by preying on the poverty of others. They didn't care that, with the exception of Redd, every debtor was one of their own grey cousins. The Nut Committee hadn't become wealthy on sentiment. But, surprised as they were, the evil trio had one consolation. The sight of Redd Squirrel standing before their long desk warmed their black souls.

The Chairman grimaced at Redd. 'Our terms are three nuts repaid for every nut loaned out,' he rapped. 'And remember, if you agree to our terms we want none of your firm paw-shakes, and gentlemen's agreements. Your word might be your bond, but ours isn't.'

'We demand things signed in red ink, and in triplicate,' added the Secretary, glaring. 'There are some who would try to rip us off if we didn't keep tight tabs.'

'And because our tabs are so tight we have never ever been swindled out of a single nut,' boasted the Vice-Chairman.

'So how many nuts do you wish to borrow, Redd Squirrel?'

'Your whole stock, if you please,' came the prompt reply.

The Chairman choked. The Vice-Chairman toppled backwards from the committee bench. The Secretary's pen-paw trembled, dripping red ink all over a pile of 'pay up or else' demands.

'But don't you live alone?' stammered the Chairman. 'We've always believed that you lived in arrogant isolation in the Grand Oak, in the middle of the wood?'

'If he doesn't live alone, then there is a mistake in my ledger,' wailed the Secretary, feverishly leafing back through his thick book. 'And a mistake written in red ink is impossible to rub out without making a terrible mess. How can I keep my ledger neat when I am fed false facts?'

'Well, it's a new one on me,' said the Vice-Chairman, frowning. 'How come the Grand Oak has the names of your illustrious family tree carved in the bark?'

'Because I live there, and alone,' said Redd, half-smiling. 'I didn't say I didn't.'

'But if you live alone, why do you need to borrow our whole stock of nuts?' said the Chairman, open-mouthed.

'If you had been keeping proper tabs you would have known that I have many brothers and sisters living in various parts of the wood,' replied Redd. 'Sadly, they were all caught out by the false spring, and are in dire need of nuts. As the head of my family I am obliged to honour my motto, which is—'

'We know,' interrupted the Chairman, rudely. 'Don't keep ramming your motto down our throats. Pardon us a moment...'

The Nut Committee went into a huddle. After a lot of head-shaking and whispering, the Chairman turned back to the patiently waiting Redd. Greed shone from his eyes as he spoke.

'The Committee agrees to loan you our full stock of nuts,' he said, 'but on new terms. Because your brothers and sisters are in such dire straits, and because your motto leaves you no choice, we have decided to turn the screw. Our new terms are: five nuts repaid for every nut loaned. Take it or leave it.'

'I'll take it,' said Redd, coolly. 'But there is one condition.'

'Almost anything,' gasped the Secretary, his head bent over his ledger, his pen scribbling furiously as he multiplied many hundreds by five in the margin, in bright red ink.

'I shall need help to carry the nuts to the foot of my Grand Oak,' said Redd. 'You see, my brothers and sisters are weak from hunger and—'

'Of course, of course,' chorused the eager Committee. In a trice, they had leapt from their fat behinds to begin gathering up pawfuls of nuts. After many puffing and panting trips to and fro, their whole hoard of nuts was finally neatly stacked at the foot of Redd's tree. After some cunning bowing and scraping before their noble customer, they took their leave. Soon they were back in their hollow tree, rubbing their paws with glee.

'Just think of the enormous profit we will make this coming autumn,' chortled the Secretary. 'And the fool signed in

triplicate, and in red ink too. The evidence in my ledger will break that over-proud squirrel. He will never be able to pay back five nuts for one in a million years.'

'He'd better,' said the grim-faced Chairman. 'For when the autumn deadline comes, we will hound and squeeze him till the pips squeak. One thing is certain, he will never look down his well-bred nose at us again.'

'I think we should celebrate this staggering business deal with a party,' whooped the Vice-Chairman. 'What say we break out some nuts from our stock, and live it up a little . . . ?'

Moments later they were beginning to realise that if they survived through the rest of the winter, they would be lucky squirrels indeed. For what was the use of a promise of wealth, when the prospects of claiming it seemed so remote? No, the evil and grasping Nut Committee would not be around that coming autumn, for at this crucial point in winter, they hadn't a nut to their name . . .

★　　★　　★

Down from the trees swarmed a horde of hungry grey squirrels. Timidly they gazed at Redd, longingly they gazed at the pile of nuts. And Redd, his smile warm, stood aside and motioned. As he listened to the happy cries of his 'brothers and sisters', he chuckled to himself. Had that trio of crooks really believed that a born and bred English red squirrel could be caught out by a false spring? But then some folk were so bent on making a fast nut that they became deafened and blinded by greed. The Honourable Redd of Ardenwood watched as the heap of nuts dwindled, snatched and borne away by many eager paws. Satisfied, his duty to his family motto done, Redd returned to his lonely home in the Grand Oak, to dream of ancient times, to await the coming of true spring . . .

DARCY THE CIRCULAR DUCK

On Tuesday morning two important things happened. Firstly, the three little ducks each received a name.

'The one with the cheeky grin we will call Duncan,' said Father. 'Which is about as posh as you can get, to my thinking.'

Duncan's lopsided grin widened as he savoured his new name.

Not to be outdone, the mother duck studied her second-born awhile. 'And this one with his pert tail will be Dudley,' she said. 'He will be set up for life with such a rich-sounding name, don't you think?'

'He will indeed,' replied Father, turning his gaze upon the smallest of the three.

The nameless duckling looked hopefully up at his parent. In the meantime, his brothers sniggered. They believed plain Dennis was plenty good enough for the weakest and the last in line.

'Darcy,' said Father. 'For his cheerful quack he will be called Darcy. Which as you know, Mother, is my own given name.'

'Quack,' said Darcy cheerfully, and he did a hop and a skip on his weak little legs.

'And with that problem solved we will all go down for our first swim,' said Mother. 'That being the second important thing this fine Tuesday morning.' And they all set off for the pool.

First into the water was Father. Next went Mother. Plop, went confident Duncan. Sploosh, went pert-tailed Dudley. Splash, went poor little Darcy, the last-born and weakest of all.

'Notice how straight as an arrow our Duncan swims,' said Mother proudly. 'He will grow up to be a natural racer one day. And observe Dudley's comical zig-zags. His sense of humour will smooth his path through life.'

'But the problem of Darcy must be faced with courage,' said Father, looking troubled. 'He is developing into what's known as a Circular Duck. He must be a throw-back, thrown forward to ruin our lives. Now what do we do?'

Together they watched as Darcy swam round and around in his aimless circles, quacking happily as his cruel brothers egged him on. No racing ever for him. Nor comical zig-zags to smooth his path through life. Just circles, large and small, but always circles, for his poor mind couldn't imagine anything else.

His parents still loved him greatly. More so than the others, for he had such a happy and trusting quack. But soon the problem of his future began to loom large.

One day, Duncan, his grin wider than ever, announced that he intended to set up home in the old canal. 'A perfect spot to practise my straight racing,' he said. Sad to see him go, but pleased for him, the parent ducks waved him goodbye.

Two days later, Dudley, his zig-zags polished and down to a fine art, declared that he had found a winding stream called Home, and intended settling there. After a few wise words from Father, a loving pat from Mother, and a happy quack from his circling brother, he vanished for ever.

'Well,' said Father, gravely, 'you know what we have to do now, don't you? About Darcy, I mean.'

'Not that,' whispered Mother. 'Anything but that. But I see your point clearly. He will never be able to fend for himself with such a circular view of life. And we won't always be here to care for him. So for Darcy it means that dreadful place, then? The place I cannot bear to mention. You say it, Father, but quietly.'

'I'm afraid it's the Home for Circular Ducks for young Darcy,' Father said, as softly as he could. 'And the sooner we get him there the better, for just look at him.'

Darcy, hopelessly trapped in his circular way of thinking, looked blissfully happy as he scooted around and around his dizzy parents. His cheerfulness was clear proof that he was completely unaware of his fate.

And so the three of them set off down the busy motorway, waddling carefully along the central white line so as to give

Darcy something straight to concentrate on.

'Honk honk' went the angry motor cars, as they swerved to avoid the little procession.

'Quack quack,' replied a cheerful Darcy, his eyes eager for a glimpse of silver water. He was anxious to begin circling again, for the straight white line made his head ache.

Late that afternoon the trio turned sharp right off the motorway, and, ignoring the ear-splitting sound of screeching motor cars, began the long walk down Leafy Lane where Darcy's destiny awaited him.

Leafy Lane plunged steeply into a small valley in which nestled Quiet Village. Once through Quiet Village the lane rose steeply again. At the top of that hill, screened by trees, was the Home for Circular Ducks. Little was known about that place except that the word 'circle' was never mentioned there. This was quite the wrong approach. Most circular ducks loved to talk about their problem, if problem it was. Few thought so. But one thing was certain. Darcy, at this very moment entering Quiet Village, would not be happy there.

The village of Quiet was a pretty place. Every cottage had a thatched roof and roses round the door. The tiny High Street boasted a Post Office that sold ice-cream, a Hatte Shoppe for old ladies to gossip in, and an Antique Parlour that sold junk. Across the road was a neatly mown green, a drinking fountain, and a comfortable bench for the old men to sit on.

But the folk of Quiet Village weren't completely happy. There was something missing from their peaceful lives. Something they all yearned for but rarely spoke about. For Quiet Village owned a beautiful round duck pond. But alas, upon its sparkling blue waters floated ... nothing. And what use a duck pond without a duck? This was the cause of the unspoken grief in Quiet Village.

Often in the past these pleasant folk had been disappointed. From time to time a passing duck had tried out their pond for comfort. But sadly, most ducks were of the racing, or zig-zag kind, and never stayed longer than to get their feet wet. So it was with renewed hope that all eyes turned upon the dismal procession entering the High Street, webbed feet precise upon the white line.

'Nearly there, and may God forgive us,' said Father, looking neither left nor right. He passed the Hatte Shoppe, ignoring the clucking sounds from the old ladies clustered about the window.

'A mere step up the hill,' wept Mother. 'There to deliver our Darcy into the Home for Circular Ducks. In short, to shift responsibility.' She looked grimly ahead.

But little Darcy wasn't in the least downcast. He had just spied the empty duck pond. With a happy quack he waddled from the white line of the road. Splash! Into the blue waters went Darcy, his thoughts purely circular, his future assured.

Small circles, large circles, loud cheerful quacks, how the folk of Quiet Village loved him! The old ladies hobbled to throw Darcy currant-bun crumbs; the old men smiled single-toothed grins from their bench, sticks tapping contentedly. And the children danced about the banks of the pond, snapping the ends from their ice-cream cones for their very own circular duck.

'Pinch me, Father,' said Mother. They had paused at the top of the hill to look back just one more time. 'It's like the end of a beautiful dream, don't you think?'

Father spoke. 'You know, Mother, it just goes to prove. So our Darcy isn't too bright. So he needs constant care and attention. But just look down there. Those folk don't care that he's a little dim, and that his mind veers towards the circular. They love him for what he is. And who knows? Perhaps one day all those Homes for Circular Ducks will be as old-fashioned as—'

'As we are,' said Mother, quietly. 'So farewell, Darcy. May you live a long and happy life.'

And Darcy did.

One day whilst on an outing, you may come across a small village. If the roofs are thatched, if there's a Post Office selling ice-cream, you will be getting warm. It just could be the village of

Quiet. Look for a Hatte Shoppe, and over the road a tidy green. There will almost certainly be a round pond beside it. Upon its waters will float a circular duck answering to the name of Darcy. And you will find that the end of your ice-cream cone will be rewarded with the happiest quack you will ever hear.

HEIL SLIM

No two brothers are exactly alike. Indeed, they can be complete opposites. Such was the case of Sam and Slim Weasel.

Sam, the eldest, had gone into the church, for he was a saintly soul and the apple of his parents' eye. Soon he had his own little chapel, and wore a tall, dignified hat. He also had a small can of scented whatsit that he swung as he walked down the aisle on Sundays. He was, as the saying goes, set up for life and smug with it. Many said that if he kept his nose clean he would make archbishop.

Slim, on the other hand, was a thoroughly nasty piece of work. Not only was he mean and vicious, but his table-manners were digusting. His mother could hardly bear to watch his performance at mealtimes. In fact, she would often excuse herself from the table, and stagger out for some fresh air.

'Must he make those gurgling noises

during the meat course?' she would complain to Father when they were alone. 'And it fair makes my stomach churn to watch good food dribbling down his grubby white vest. And all that horrid talk during pudding. All that nonsense about rubbing folk out. And why does he wear that ugly armband, and continually sharpen his little stone axe? But it is the terrible rages that unnerve me. What will be the outcome of it all, I'd like to know?'

Father had no answers at all. Frankly, he was petrified of his son Slim, and with good reason. Slim's threats, and he made a lot, weren't idle ones. No one was safe when Slim was in an ugly mood. It so happened he was in one now. This explained why his parents were hiding beneath a bush outside the family cave. Trembling, their eyes rolling in terror, they were listening to the cursing and the sound of smashed crockery coming from within.

'He had Granny half over that steep cliff yesterday,' wept Mother. 'And her with legs like jelly on two sticks. Luckily, she managed to cling onto a bit of crag until he had calmed down. And she so fond of him, too.'

'He's a wrong 'un and no mistake,' agreed Father. 'He's picked up some bad blood from somewhere. From your side, no doubt. I've tried to discuss his future with him but he won't listen. I even suggested that he might follow his brother Sam into the church. It's about time Slim carved out a career for himself instead of smashing all the supper plates. Just listen to that din in there.'

'And what about that rolling boulder last week?' said Mother, her eyes watering as she remembered.

'One thing is certain,' said Father. 'Boulders don't roll down hills on their own. It's a good thing I spotted it coming. Hello, I said, there's a huge boulder rolling down on top of me. Luckily, it only struck me a glancing blow.'

'It's a miracle your body wasn't crushed out of shape.' Tears flowed from Mother's soft brown eyes. 'Are you certain Slim was behind it?'

'Behind the boulder, no doubt about it,' replied her husband. 'Not that Slim would admit it. I questioned him about it when I returned from the first-aid point. Son, I said, were you behind the boulder business?'

'And behind Granny on the cliff edge,' his wife reminded him. 'And what did Slim have to say for himself?'

'He merely shouted, "Sieg Heil", or some such nonsense. Come on, Slim, son, I said, you can do better than that. Own up and we'll forget all about it. Then he said it, all sullen...'

'What did Slim say all sullen?' asked Mother, mopping at her eyes and trying to perk up.

'He said he was practising,' mused Father. 'But practising for what, I asked him? I was quite insistent, considering how frightened of him I am.'

Mother interrupted. 'As his father you have a perfect right to ask Slim what he is practising for. After all, practice makes perfect, and who knows where that could lead? Did Slim make any kind of reply?'

'He said when he hears "the call" we will know about it,' said Father, looking perplexed. 'Then he smiled secretly, and

81

began to sharpen his little stone axe. Frankly, Mother, I didn't like Slim's attitude one little bit. One thing is certain, he's not practising to follow his brother Sam into the church. Pity though, for he would look smart in a tall hat, and swinging a can of scented whatsit.'

'Slim wouldn't be allowed in with that little stone axe of his,' said Mother, firmly. She became weepy again. 'I didn't tell you, but Sam was followed into the church by Slim only last Sunday. "Slim," I shouted, all shocked and shook-up, and running down the aisle, "what are you going to do to your brother in this sacred place?"'

'Slim actually attacked his brother Sam?' said Father, aghast. 'And Sam in his tall hat, too . . . ?'

'Half-way down his throat,' whispered Mother. 'Slim had shoved Sam's little can of scented whatsit half-way down his brother's throat. Why all this violence, Slim, said I, trying to rescue Sam from those strong mad paws.'

'I'll bet your Slim screamed that he

was practising,' said Father, nodding wisely. Suddenly he jumped into the air as a twig snapped behind him. 'Crikey O'Reilly,' he gasped. 'I thought for a moment that Slim was creeping up behind us.'

'Where's Slim?' gabbled Mother, peering about. 'No, it can't be. I can hear him wolfing down a whole rice pudding in our cave. Don't frighten me like that, Father. In my breast I suddenly felt the flim-flams rising. For a brief moment my gorge was choked with fear.' She began to weep again. 'Why, oh why, did we decide to live here with all boulders balanced on hills, and Slim creeping about amongst the cracks and crannies? Slim is a disgrace to us, with his bad blood from your side. How I wish he had some gentle ambition to set his sights on.'

'I'm afraid Slim's ambition is to practise till perfect, in readiness for when "the call" comes,' replied Father, sighing heavily. 'But until then, Slim's hobby is slinking about with mad eyes, and keeping his little stone axe razor-sharp ... Hark—what was that frightening noise?'

They held their breaths, listening intently.

'He's started on the cold cuts I was saving for supper,' whispered Mother. 'I can hear his savage teeth grinding on the bits of bone. Quick, Father, go into the cave and forbid Slim. Why can't you be a firm father instead of a coward, terrified out of his wits by his own mad son? Why won't you summon up some courage and go rescue the cold cuts? March in and chase him out of my pantry and say, "Keep out of your mother's pantry, Slim." Tell him that his brother Sam, who took to the church like a duck to water, will be over directly to read him a sermon from his big thick book.'

'I wouldn't enter that cave for all the tea in China,' said Father, with a shudder. 'And if our son Sam, who will make archbishop if he keeps off the strong Holy Water, so much as put one paw inside, he would be cold cuts before he had time to swing his little can. Leave well alone, Mother. Let Slim sort out his problems in his own way. All I hope is that he doesn't find that jug of Holy

Water Sam gave us. That would put the cat amongst the pigeons.'

'Crikey O'Reilly,' sobbed Mother. 'Just listen to the fresh bout of violence taking place in our home. The smashing and screaming is becoming unbearable. Could it be our Slim is searching for the blancmange I hid on the top pantry shelf to set? Why don't you rush inside with a heavy rock and try to hit his head with it, Father? Is it fair that he should be wolfing cold cuts and blancmange while we sit shaking with fear outside?'

'Hush,' said Father, his ears cocked. 'It's suddenly gone all quiet in there. Apart from the odd stealthy rustle, our son Slim seems to have settled down. Now's your chance, Mother. Go in and rescue what's left of our supper. If he stirs while you are in there, run as fast as you can for the entrance, not forgetting to snatch up the jug of strong Holy Water. In the meantime, I'll stay here and try to work out what went wrong with the lad, his brother having taken to the church . . .'

'Like a duck to water,' finished Mother, her voice filled with wonderment. 'But you are right, Father. Sitting here trembling won't solve any problems. I'll creep in softly, perhaps he's asleep.'

Just as she reached the entrance of the cave so the screaming started up again. She fled back beneath the bush.

'Look out,' warned Father ducking his head. 'Here comes our son Slim . . .'

A spitting, snarling fury burst forth from the cave. Mother and Father watched in fascinated horror as Slim, or rather the blur of unleashed energy that was Slim, flashed past them, heading for the hills.

'What ails you, Slim, son?' yelled Father sympathetically. 'Was it us? Did we fail you somewhere along the way?'

'Did you leave a cold cut or two for your father's supper?' shrilled Mother.

Slim paused on the skyline. From a crag he hurled words, nasty violent words, their meaning clear only to his own black soul. 'It's the world . . . I hate the world . . . But the day will come when millions will follow me . . . Then I will destroy the world, and everything in it . . .' Then he swore mightily and vanished over the crest.

'You know that lad's not so daft,' said Father, settling down with the jug of Holy Water. 'I can't say I care for it much myself. Still, we can be grateful that Slim has finished his practising. He must be pretty well perfect by now. Though perfect for what, I dread to think.'

Together they entered the now quiet cave.

'What don't you care for much?' asked Mother, gathering the remains of the cold cuts from the floor.

'The world,' replied Father. 'What's it done for us I'd like to know?'

'It gave our son Sam a tall hat, and a little church of his own,' she reminded him. 'Though how it will treat Slim running wild in the hills, I can't imagine. Not kindly, I'm sure, for he hasn't even a few table-manners to fall back on.'

'My worry is, what will Slim do to the world?' said Father, pondering between swigs of Holy Water. 'Don't forget he is a nasty piece of work, son or no son. But come, let us count our blessings, as our son Sam would say. Slim's gone, that's the main thing. Strange though, but he never took his toys. He thought the world of his armband, and his little sharp axe... Crikey O'Reilly, what's that coming down the hill at full speed, and screaming?'

'It's Slim come back to make our lives hell again,' wailed Mother. 'Quick, run for our son Sam. Tell him to come as fast as he can, and to wear his tall hat.'

'What a lousy world it is out there,' spat a wild-eyed Slim, snatching up Father's cold cuts and stuffing them into his mouth. 'Where are my toys, I'll be needing 'em...'

'You've only been away five minutes. How can you say it's a lousy world after only five minutes?' yelled Father, dashing from the cave, closely followed by Mother. Outside in the cold they crouched beneath the bush, warily watching the mouth of the cave. There was a lot of noisy rummaging going on inside. Also, ominously, came the sound of a little stone axe being sharpened.

'I think Slim has received the "call" he was waiting for,' remarked Mother uneasily. 'I think he has decided upon a career at last.'

'*Sieg Heil*,' bawled Slim from the depths of the cave.

'That does it,' said Father grimly. 'Call or no call, it's about time we took Slim in hand. We owe it to the world, Mother. We will be firm and guide him into a nice safe career where he can't do any harm. Like his brother Sam who took to the church...'

'Like a duck to water,' agreed Mother. 'A career where he won't need his sharp little axe.'

There was no longer any need of words. They were thinking along similar lines.

Together they climbed the hill above the cave. Working swiftly, for Slim was liable to emerge any moment to begin his nasty life's work, they began to roll boulders down the slope, not ceasing until the mouth of the cave was well and truly blocked. Only then did they return back down the hill.

'Slim, son,' called Father, craning his ears to the sounds of fury that drifted from the sealed entrance. 'Forgive us, but we think this is for the best.'

'*Sieg Heil,*' came the muffled bellow from within.

Mother nodded sadly. They were doing the right thing, of that she was sure.

'Your career is all arranged, son,' shouted Father. 'It's called being a hermit, and dedicating yourself to the simple life. Do you hear me, Slim, son?'

Slim did. He could see as well, for Father could just make out the savage red glow of his son's eyes through a gap between the boulders.

'We'll push in some cold cuts and blancmange from time to time,' called Mother encouragingly. 'And we will arrange for Sam to come and read to you from his big thick book. And swing his little can of scented whatsit, whenever he's steady enough on his paws because of the Holy Water. You'll enjoy being a hermit, you see if you won't. You will take to it just like your brother Sam took to his career . . .'

'*Sieg Heil,*' screamed Slim, trying to poke his sharp little axe through the crack between the boulders.

'Like a duck to water...' agreed Father, turning away.

THE SONG OF THE SOUTHERN TREE-CLIMBER

There are many types of beetle in England. Some are beautiful, others quite drab. Some can fly, others cannot, nor want to. Beetles have their differences, and rightly so. They wouldn't have it any other way. But there is one difference of such importance that it needs to be mentioned.

The Shady Wood was home for many kinds of beetle. Some lived amongst the rotting leaves on the ground, others high in the tree-tops. Stubby-winged, rainbow-winged, multi-eyed, or of the plain, brown peering kind, they all had one thing in common. They were Midland beetles. They were Warwickshire born and bred beetles. They were 'Shakespeare country' beetles, and proud of it, from the tips of their sensitive antennae, to the soles of their various feet. And the Shady Wood rang to their song, or hushed for the lone voice chanting verse that a long night's brood had inspired.

Far to the south lived their cousins. These were bright and witty beetles, masters of the popular bawdy ballad. Theirs was the hustle and bustle, and they revelled in their quick, slick way of life. Soon the twain would meet, in, of all sacred places, the Shady Wood.

It was a freak gale that snatched the Southern Tree-climber from his Hyde Park home, bore him northwards, and dumped him in the middle of Shady Wood. It was the first time he had flown and he enjoyed the experience very much. For the first time in his life he wished he had wings of his own. It was also the last, for he was much too cheerful a beetle to fret about what might have been. After a snappy rendering of 'Maybe it's because I'm a Londoner', he settled down in this 'hick, back-water place', and waited for the next gale home.

The Southern Tree-climber had three loves. One, an enormous appetite for garlic, two, a zest for climbing trees, and three, the song he sang as he climbed them. He was in luck. There was lots of wild garlic growing in Shady Wood, and trees were plentiful indeed. So within an hour of arriving he was full to bursting, exercising his powerful lungs, and sizing up his first tree. Approaching the tall elm he took firm hold on its bark. Then, very determinedly, and with a comical rolling gait, he began to climb.

'I am climbing up a tree . . .' he sang, settling into a nice swinging rhythm. For a moment he paused to adjust his grip.

'Climbing up a tree, that's me . . .' he yelled, continuing upwards.

'Rain or shine, I'll always be . . .

'Climbing up a tree,' he finished, these last notes and words loud and triumphant in the hush of Shady Wood.

The inhabitants of this genteel place were startled out of their wits. A few fell over on to their backs, wriggling helplessly until flipped back over by kind friends. Others fainted dead away, their sensitive hearing shocked by the coarse and bawdy song. Soon the area about the elm became thronged with refined Midland beetles, most of them

still unable to believe their ears. Curiously, fearfully, they gazed at the Southern Tree-climber who, by this time, was a foot or so up the tree, and taking not the slightest notice of the onlookers. He appeared to be limbering up. Twice he cleared his throat ... 'mi mi mi mi' he warbled, opera-singer style. Drab he might be, but there was no doubting his sublimely happy confidence. If the folk of Shady Wood were hoping ... but no, for such thoughts were quickly dashed.

'I am climbing up a tree ...' he began again, his voice and the sway of his rump in perfect time.

'Climbing up a tree that's me ...

'Rain or shine, I'll always be ...

'Climbing up a tree!' This last joyous bellow found him twice as high as before, and looking eagerly upwards.

By this time the beetles of Shady Wood had guessed the worst. Country folk they might be, but stupid they were not. They could reason quite logically when they weren't composing sweet tunes and poignant verses. They had already calculated that the elm tree was about fifty feet high. That worked out at one awful song per foot, times fifty, according to the southerner's rate of climb. They had also worked out the time factor. The pest would reach the top of the tree about midday. Hours away. No, it was unthinkable. Surely he would tire and take his nuisance elsewhere? But these simple beetles would never understand the relentless reasoning of this common cousin from the south.

'I am climbing up a tree . . .' Off he went again, stubbornly cheerful, his song even louder than before.

Deeply distressed, the beetles of Shady Wood prayed for midday to arrive. Their jangled nerves were now at snapping point, as that ferocious song echoed down through the thick foliage of the elm. And then, at long last, the sun stood directly over the wood. A blessed silence reigned. There was in the air a stillness so complete that it could almost be touched. The Shady Wood beetles, many driven quite out of their minds, basked in that total absence of sound . . .

'I am climbing down a tree . . .' yelled the Southern Tree-climber. At this point three rare species of beetle left immediately for foreign parts.

'Climbing down a tree, that's me . . .' The information fell mostly on deaf ears. The listeners and watchers were scrambling for cover, burying their heads beneath anything that would shut out that awful din.

'Rain or shine, I'll always be . . .' But a strange thing was happening. The feet and end portions of various types of young beetle were beginning to tap and sway. Heads filled with anger were losing control of bodies responding to rhythm. The youth of Shady Wood were becoming infected. Some were already emerging from cover and were choosing trees. A few were equipped for climbing, others not. Some were natural singers, some quite tone-deaf. But their enthusiasm was boundless. For they all agreed that this new and popular music from the south knocked their dreamy old ballads into a cocked hat. The strident beat, the easy-to-remember words, this was definitely their scene.

And suddenly the generation gap yawned and yawned as an old way of life passed forever.

'We are climbing up a tree . . .' sang the young of Shady Wood, delighting in the knowledge that one didn't need a trained voice to express the mood of this glorious new sound. After a practice scramble or two, they gathered in excited discussion. 'Climbing down a tree . . .' ended the puzzled Southern Tree-climber. For a while he sat at the foot of the elm, scratching his head. Who were all these strange beetles? And why were they swarming up trees and singing his song? But then, imitation was a form of flattery he supposed with a shrug. Still bewildered but ever cheerful, he hopped across to a promising looking oak. It would do fine for tomorrow, he thought, glancing up. Sighing, he settled down to sleep amongst its roots.

But sleep would not come. For a long time he lay tossing and turning. The oak, he calculated, had to be at least one hundred feet high. He would need to start very early in the morning to climb it by midday. And there was his reputation to consider. What with all these country beetles copying him, he couldn't let the south down. He decided there was no time like the present. Scrambling to his feet he gripped the bark of the massive trunk . . .

'I am climbing up a tree . . .' His joyous song echoed once again through Shady Wood. He climbed in a darkness silvered by a high riding moon. But to the north, huge storm clouds were gathering. By morning the weather would have swung around, carrying hurricane force gales. By midday they would be blasting southwards, snatching up and bearing homewards one who had destroyed a way of life . . .

'Climbing up a tree, that's me . . .'

Here today, gone tomorrow, but it was much too late. The seeds had been sown. The youth of Shady Wood had tasted the joys of self-expression. In the morning and in the days to come, they would begin to experiment, to compose small ear-splitting works of their own. Soon cults would arise, and the dreamy ballads of Shakespeare country would be scoffed at, would be sung only by the very old who remembered a time— 'Climbing up a tree!' bellowed the merry Southern Tree-climber—a tranquil time, before he came . . .

AND ZIGGY MAKES FOUR

As usual, the giraffes were sitting in their early morning circle enjoying the sunrise. As usual, they were singing their favourite song. It was called 'On a clear day you can see for ever', and being fine singers, the giraffes did full justice to it. But this morning the old group leader had more important things on his mind than song. He had been nervous and touchy for some days now. The other giraffes agreed that he had completely lost his sense of humour. And they all knew why. Firstly, he had developed a worrying limp. Secondly, a certain youngster had begun playing practical jokes on him. The culprit's name was Ziggy.

Now Ziggy had been attending school for just four days. But those four days had changed him from a shy, tongue-tied infant, into a mischievous prankster. For the old group leader, enough was enough from young Ziggy. This morning he had reached the end of his tether. As soon as the singing was over (he was proud of his fine deep voice) he called for order. He had a few words to say before the youngsters went off to school.

'I will speak of this only once,' he said. 'And then, hopefully, the matter will be closed for ever. I will be blunt but kindly. I am referring, of course, to the astonishing change that has come over our once-polite young Ziggy.'

'I should like to draw attention to my son's hazel eyes,' said Ziggy's mother, quickly. 'They are his outstanding feature, and should be taken into consideration.'

'His good looks are not in question,' the old group leader replied. 'What worries me is his practical joking.'

'The blame lies at the door of The School over the Hill,' everyone agreed. 'We have noticed that the happiest days of Ziggy's life are turning into a nightmare for others.'

'His latest prank, for instance,' continued the group leader. 'In the dead of last night didn't we hear him shout at the top of his voice, "lions, four of 'em", causing us to scramble to our feet as quickly as possible?'

'You last of all, I noticed,' said Ziggy's mother. 'But with a limp like yours I'm not surprised. But surely my son is entitled to have high spirits? I take it you intend to tick Ziggy off? So tick him off, and let's have done with it.'

The group leader shifted to ease his painful leg. He went on. 'I have been your leader for three years now—'

'Four,' said little Ziggy, in a firm voice.

His mother hastened to explain. 'As you know, yesterday was his fourth day at school, where he learned all about fours. Today he is studying fives. That's if he ever arrives at The School over the Hill. How long will this lecture last, I wonder?'

'Until Ziggy sees the error of his ways,' retorted the old group leader. 'I intend to make an example of him. But never fear, I will chide him as gently as possible. I want him to realise how lucky he is to have schooling. For myself I only had three days, and that was my lot.'

Ziggy's mother snorted angrily. 'You

wish to publicly ridicule my son, is that it? Just because he has learned about fours, and has picked up a sense of humour at The School over the Hill.'

'I am ordering Ziggy to stand upon his three legs, and apologise,' came the sharp reply.

'Four,' corrected Ziggy, adjusting his striped school cap.

'Soon he'll be on the high numbers,' remarked his proud mother. 'That's if you'll allow him to snatch up his satchel, and get off. Or are you determined to deny him a proper education?'

'I would not be so cruel,' protested the group leader. 'But surely when the young play practical jokes I am entitled to put them in their place? Isn't this why you voted me leader in the first place, to keep order? Isn't this why you intend to vote me in again in three days' time, on polling day?'

'That's if those two lions behind that bush don't ruin your plans,' said the group leader's bitter rival. 'And don't accuse me of practical joking, for I received schooling myself when I was young. Having attended The School

over the Hill for two full days, I say there are two fierce lions behind that bush.'

'Four,' said Ziggy. He yawned as he always did when afraid.

'Very well,' snapped his mother. 'If it will get him to school on time I will nudge my son to his feet. If you can't take a joke, so be it. But if you ask me it's that limp of yours that's preying on your mind. Ziggy—'

Hastily, little Ziggy scrambled to his feet. He had no wish to be nudged. A fellow pupil had nudged him three times in school the day before, and it had hurt very much. He had expected to feel a fourth nudge, but the other wasn't very bright.

'Now, young Ziggy,' said the stern group leader. 'What have you to say for yourself? And never mind staring at that bush that my rival said had two lions behind it. And straighten that cap.'

Obediently Ziggy adjusted his striped cap, his wide hazel eyes intent upon a waving bush a few yards away. He began to yawn again, and again . . .

'Don't you realise that shouting "lions, four of 'em" in the dead of night is wrong, Ziggy?' lectured the old group leader. 'And please stop staring at that bush and yawning, when I'm talking to you. If there were three lions behind it we would soon know.'

'Four,' said Ziggy, beginning to fidget.

By this time all the giraffes were becoming restless. They began to mutter, many already on their feet, and sniffing the air. The rival wasn't even sniffing, he was sure about the contents of the bush. Painfully, the old group leader staggered to stand upright. For himself he was convinced it was a false alarm. Perhaps even a ruse to distract him from the ticking-off he continued to give Ziggy.

'Why do you brow-beat my son this way?' shouted Mother. 'For all we know he may be right about those lions. Four of them, if they squeezed together, could easily hide behind that bush.'

'So why are we wasting time?' said the leader's rival, nervously. 'I don't want to be around when those two lions burst from that bush.'

'Four,' insisted Ziggy, snatching up

his satchel, and dashing off in the direction of The School over the Hill. Suddenly maddened with fear, the rest of the group followed hard on his heels. At that moment the old leader saw three lions bound from the bush in pursuit. But giraffes have extremely long legs. They soon left the lions exhausted and panting far behind. The old group leader heaved a sigh of relief. How lucky he hadn't attempted to flee with the rest. With his worrying limp, who knows what might have happened? Thankfully he hobbled over to the bush and sank down beneath its shade. There he would await the group's return. And when Ziggy came home from school that evening he would receive another lecture on the folly of practical joking.

'All that schooling, and the youngster can't get his sums right,' the oldster sighed. 'For since when did three lions make four?'

There was a stealthy movement from the depths of the bush. Then a flash of tawny yellow. A bird? A patch of sun-dappled sand. Sums are very hard to learn. Did Ziggy get his right? Let's hope not. Let's hope he does better with is fives . . .

GOOD NEIGHBOURS

'There is nothing quite like moving house,' said Polly, shutting the front door for the last time. 'Especially when one is moving up a notch. Not that we will become snobs. But we have the children to think about, and the city is such a rough place these days. They say Solihull is the only place to live.'

'The only place for snails with ambition,' agreed Oliver, her husband. 'We will make a go of it, I'm sure. There is nothing snobbish about wanting to better oneself. We will build a nice little house with a sunshine roof in Solihull, like those folk in the upper bracket. Why should our children have to spend the rest of their lives in this dump? No, Polly, we will give them a good start like what we never had.'

'After all,' said Polly, indignantly, 'why shouldn't our sons wear school caps with badges on? And who says our daughters can't wear ostrich-feather hats that you wear to Balls, where you whirl round and round like nobody's business? Why should we, who have always sounded our aitches, be forced to live amongst these city whizz-kids?'

'No whizz-kids for our daughters,' said Oliver firmly. 'For them, wall-to-wall carpet will be as natural as can be. And with a sunshine roof, why, the swells of Solihull will be falling over themselves to escort them to swank do's. So come, let us leave this dreadful place with all the rude poems on the walls, and mingle amongst the cream of society where we rightfully belong. Remember now, single file along the gutter. And tell our Gwennie to shout in little Daniel's ear. Tell her to tell him that we will get his hearing fixed by a Solihull specialist after we have got the sunshine roof sorted out . . .'

Little Daniel looked delighted as he took his place at the end of the procession. The youngest of five, he crawled happily along behind his sister, Gwennie, his neglected ears cocked for the sound of on-coming traffic. His shell glowed in the sunshine, for it had been highly polished for the occasion.

'Good riddance,' yelled an old neighbour. 'We are going to throw a big party to celebrate.'

'Ignore 'em,' advised Oliver. 'Shout to little Daniel to cock a snook.'

The little snail soon got the idea. He was still cocking his snook as they crossed the boundary line into Solihull.

Wicket gates and winding leafy lanes. There was no doubting the taste of the residents of Solihull. Everything unseemly was banished from public view. And everywhere, even down to the gutters, there was an air of quiet, well-ordered pride. No whizz-kids with slogan-daubed shells here. Polly and Oliver, the older children in the middle, and little deaf Daniel at the rear, paused entranced.

'We've arrived!' shouted Oliver. 'If we don't build a home in this quiet little dell my name is Trevor. All together now—What is it?'

'Perfect!' chorused the family.

'And what isn't allowed here?'

'Coarse language and whizz-kids,' came the rehearsed reply.

'Eh?' said little deaf Daniel.

'And now to build our dream home,' continued Oliver. 'What will the little sign on swinging chains say, Gwennie?'

'Duncrawlin,' piped the youngest daughter. 'For I am artistic, and in charge of the paint-brush.'

'And now,' said a solemn Oliver, 'let us chip in as a close-knit family, and make our new home something more than bricks and mortar. Let it be filled with love and laughter. And don't look now but we are being clocked by a nosy new neighbour. Take no notice, for our motto is to keep ourselves to ourselves. Just wait until we get our sunshine roof on. Our nosy new neighbours will be green with envy for I see their houses are much of a muchness, and red-tiled to the last one. Right, children, scatter about and search for the best materials to build our new home. What is our first watchword?'

'Taste!' they all shouted. 'For we are no longer ordinary snails, but posh Gastropods.'

'Eh?' said little deaf Daniel.

'And what is our second, but equally important watchword?' prompted

Oliver.

'Good neighbourliness!' came the cry.

'Taste!' yelled little deaf Daniel, wondering where the ear specialist had got to. He hadn't understood that the sunshine roof came first.

But at last the building of the new home got underway.

'That's a mistake for a start,' said the nosy new neighbour, watching the sunshine roof go on. 'And what's the idea pinching the bricks from my outhouse? It just fell down, thanks to you lot. What are you, vandals or something?'

'I thought there were no whizz-kids in Solihull,' sighed Polly. 'I hope this one doesn't live next door.'

'Three down, actually,' replied the neighbour. 'The house that had the red door. Why have you pinched my red front door, I wonder? Don't you know it's against the law? And why are your children rampaging all over the Dell, stealing anything that takes their fancy?'

Oliver looked angry. 'One can't build a dream home without materials,' he snapped. 'Anyway, that outhouse looked ready to fall down. You should have kept it in better repair.'

The neighbour sucked at his pipe. 'That's as maybe,' he said. 'But I might as well warn you that the Dell Committee has just held a meeting. They are agreed that your manners are deplorable. We, that is the Dell Committee, have always tried to stop the riff-raff moving into this area. I see we haven't succeeded.'

'I'll have you know we were highly respected in the city,' bristled Oliver. 'Folk stepped aside when they saw us coming.'

'That doesn't surprise me,' replied the neighbour. He re-lit his pipe, and puffed away thoughtfully.

'Would the smoky gentleman be the ear specialist?' enquired little Daniel. 'Or has he come to fit us for school caps with badges on?'

'What you see is a whizz-kid smoking a pipe,' retorted Oliver. 'I'll bet his girls don't get invited to swanky Balls and things. Remember, children, there are no swells three doors down.'

'We've learned one thing,' said Polly,

quite shocked. 'There are whizz-kids even in posh Solihull. I wouldn't be surprised if his wife wore a flowered hat, and talked down her nose. I hope she doesn't drop in for my coffee mornings. Phonies I just can't take.'

'My wife happens to be the Chair-person of the Dell Committee,' replied the angry neighbour, knocking out his pipe. 'So she wears a flowered hat and talks down her nose, what's it to do with you?'

'I think the smoky gentleman has got the hump,' said little deaf Daniel. 'He hasn't once looked down my ears.'

'I was going to lend you my lawn-mower,' the neighbour went on. 'But I'm thinking twice about it now. I was prepared to help as a good neighbour should, but what did I get—my out-house knocked down, and my red front door stolen?'

'Have you quite finished?' said Oliver. He turned to his family. 'Righto, inside, everyone. Despite this interfering pest "Duncrawlin" is completed.'

'Don't say I didn't try to warn you

about that sunshine roof,' said the neighbour from three doors down, lighting up his pipe again. He pointed the stem at little deaf Daniel. 'And if I were you I'd get an ear specialist to look at that small chap. I notice he cranes to hear what's being said.'

'Now he advises us on medical matters,' said a haughty Polly, herding the children inside their new red front door. 'Not to mention that he sneers about our lack of a lawn-mower. Well, let me tell him this. If I see a flowered hat marching down our drive, I'll kick it up in the air.'

'You'd do that to the Chair-person of the Dell Committee?' yelled the neighbour. 'Right, expect a Round Robin anytime.' With that he stormed off.

'What's a Round Robin?' asked Gwennie, shutting the door on the world. 'And can I hang the name of our house on its swinging chains now, Dad? It's nearly dry.'

'A Round Robin is a snooty way to drive us out of the district,' snorted Oliver. 'If I'm not mistaken we will soon see a flowered hat marching up and down the Dell drives, collecting signed complaints about us.'

'And us only here a day or so,' wept Polly, peering through the window-frame that they had wrenched from the wall of number two. 'Our new neighbours have certainly got off to a bad start. Fancy trying to drive us out without trying to get to know us properly. Well, we are not moving again. Here we are and here we stay.'

'Can I go out and kick things?' asked little Daniel hopefully. 'Or should I wait until the ear specialist has been and gone?'

'I suggest we all get a good night's sleep,' said Oliver. 'For I have an idea we will be having trouble with that lot in the morning.'

'That's the first time I've ever seen a whizz-kid smoking a pipe,' said Polly. 'You certainly live and learn in this funny world.'

'Eh?' said little deaf Daniel. He settled down to dream about the greenhouse he had spied whilst peeping over next-door's garden wall. He had already hidden a pile of smooth pebbles. The loud clatter of breaking glass was one of the few sounds his weak ears could pick up. He was looking forward to the morning . . .

*   *   *

'Put that light out,' bawled Oliver. It was the beginning of a terrible night for him and his brood.

'I warned you about that sunshine roof,' called the neighbour from three doors down. 'But would you listen?'

'And I've collected two full sheets of signed complaints,' shrilled a lady's voice.

It was the lamp-post that was causing all the trouble. Or rather, the bright yellow light on top of it. It was glaring down through the sunshine roof, and dazzling the eyes of Oliver and his family. Sleep was impossible.

'I can't stand much more of this,' wept Polly. 'We'll be physical wrecks by the morning. And there's us needing to be alert in case we get stabbed in the back. Can't little Daniel climb up and smash it to bits or something?'

'If that lot out there were anything like neighbours, they'd come and help!' shouted Oliver into the night. 'We've all got red-rimmed eyes in here. Not a one of us has had a wink of sleep to speak of.'

'Blame yourselves,' came the triumphant reply. 'We were prepared to be good neighbours but what did you do? You stole our front doors, ripped up our prize roses to plant in your new garden, and knocked down an out-house three doors down. You can go hang for all we care.'

'Does that mean the ear specialist won't be calling?' asked little Daniel tearfully.

'It means we are on the move again,' said a grim Polly. 'Whizz-kids, that's all that lot are. It's the same everywhere we go. Never once have we been lucky enough to find good neighbours. I'm beginning to think there is no such thing. For where are they when we need them? Tucked up in bed smoking their pipes, that's where they are. Come on, we are going.'

A loud cheer arose from the residents

of the Dell.

'Good riddance!' shouted the nosy neighbour from three doors down. 'And before you go, bring my red front door back!'

It was a sad family who assembled in the gutter beneath the glaring light of that lamp-post. In the lead was Oliver. Just behind came Polly. Then came the in-between children, crying and rubbing their smarting eyes. Last but one was young Gwennie, clutching her newly-painted 'Duncrawlin' sign, and sniffling softly. Bringing up the rear was little Daniel, having heard next to nothing of the arguments of the previous day. And he still couldn't understand what had happened to the famous ear specialist.

'Cheltenham Spa is supposed to be a friendly place,' said Oliver. 'Shall we give it a try?'

'Well, one thing is certain,' said Polly as they set off. 'There won't be any whizz-kids there. If there are any good neighbours in the world, we'll find them in Cheltenham Spa.'

'Are there any ear specialists in Cheltenham Spa?' called Gwennie. 'For little Daniel just said that he is beginning to believe in Santa Claus more.'

'Ear specialists are ten a penny in Cheltenham Spa,' replied Oliver airily. 'As plentiful as good neighbours, so I've heard. Shout to little Daniel that as soon as the sunshine roof is fixed, his problem will have priority . . .'

Meanwhile the Gastropods of posh Cheltenham Spa were sleeping peacefully. Never in their wildest dreams could they have foreseen just what was bearing down on their peaceful town. They were soon to find out.

THE KEY TO HAPPINESS

He owned three bottle-tops, a twist of silver paper, and a Christmas bell. Because he was so poor he and his family lived in Lower Glade amongst others of his kind.

The wealthy lived in Upper Glade. These magpies shunned their poorer neighbours for they feared poverty as death itself. In their eyes to sink so low could only be an illness, and illnesses were catching. So they kept their own company and distance.

But despite his poverty the magpie of Lower Glade was a hopeful bird. Life was not so bad. There was food in plenty, he had a devoted family, and there were neighbours, always friendly and helpful in a crisis. And he had his burning ambition which never faltered. For he knew that somewhere lay the key to true happiness, and one day he, the poor magpie, would find it. But in the meantime he held his small treasures up to the sun, and fancied them priceless beyond measure.

But the poor magpie still found it hard to contain his envy. He and his family lived in a careless pile of twigs at the top of a tree. At night-time he would gaze at the stars. Precious jewels against the velvet black of space, they seemed to mock his lowly state. How he envied their owner his hoard. How noble and mighty that rich one, to display such wealth so openly. And the poor magpie would sigh, tuck from view his rusting bottle-tops, his twist of paper and the Christmas bell, to sleep a fretful night away. But with the morning came hope yet again.

His search for the key to happiness took him far and wide. Many days he spent amongst the Black Hills, his eyes ever bright and watchful for the glittering prize that would raise him above his peers. Along the banks of racing streams he flapped, his hopes often raised and dashed by the flash of sun on crystal water. But he never gave up the search, for he believed that the key to happiness awaited a magpie as miserably poor as he, and would reveal itself in its own good time.

One day his quest took him in through an open window. In wonder he gazed at the treasure, spread out before his beady eyes. And the thief in him ached for the small golden bauble, its single gemstone fired by a shaft of sunlight. For it was the key to happiness, could be nothing else, and was rightfully his. Taking it to him he fled, his breast splashed with crimson from the reflected light of that single stone. For the key to happiness outshone even the harvest sun.

Now he was the richest of magpies. Three bottle-tops, a twist of silver paper, and a Christmas bell, all were cast aside. Displayed upon the careless twigs was the key to happiness, gold and bright, its glowing gem dazzling the many envious eyes. Proud and boastful now, he and his family looked down upon the poor magpies of Lower Glade. They who once had shared his poverty, had gladly offered friendship, were despised and shunned. And the reproach in their eyes made the once poor magpie shrill and petty, for he who possessed the key to happiness was now all-powerful.

At last he had everything he had ever yearned for. Wealth, position, and such new friends as he deserved, all were his. His life became a social whirl and he loved every moment of it. The move to Upper Glade was a pinnacle reached. Triumphantly, the key to happiness gripped firmly in his beak, he left his humble home; he believed for ever. And how sweet was revenge. How the bowing and the scraping of his rich friends pleased him. His every wish was their command, and his spirits shone bright, as the key to happiness . . . dulled.

Its golden sheen was peeling. The gemstone once so dazzling to the eye glowed sullenly now, until one day it ceased to glow at all. Rust set in as the acid rains ate through the surface glitter, revealing the base metal beneath. And new friends, seeing this, grew distant and cold. Only then did the magpie realise that the key to happiness was false, and that the real one had eluded him yet again. Later, despised and rejected, he saw the truth clearly. And he was filled with remorse and regret.

He had sought for the key to happiness in far-off places, lusted for the status he thought it would bring, and it had decayed before his eyes.

The poor magpie picked from the ground three bottle-tops, a twist of silver paper, and a Christmas bell. He laid them carefully upon a careless pile of twigs. Here in Lower Glade, surrounded by his real friends so poor but true, he looked up at the stars. There was no envy in his gaze now. He felt at peace beneath their beauty. And the key to happiness was everywhere about him.

TOP OF THE HEAP

Ants practise a rigid class system. At the top of the heap is the Queen. If she chooses to wear a crown as high as St Paul's Cathedral it is not to be questioned, for her role in the colony is vital. She is the life force and can do pretty much what she wants. But directly beneath her are the many layers of society. Contrary to popular belief, this teeming society is a den of intrigue and back-stabbing. It is nonsense to suggest that every ant knows his place and keeps to it for the good of the whole. The fact is, ant colonies are notorious for getting it wrong when it comes to dishing out jobs. Take the case of James...

For as long as he could remember James had staggered about beneath heavy loads of Precious Supplies. For an ant born with a bad back this was hardly the career he was best suited for. And that was not all. The case of James threw up an even greater stupidity in this class-ridden society. Though born with a bad back, James had been compensated. His was the brain of a lofty genius, and any fool should have realised that he would have been better employed solving difficult problems instead of straining his delicate back muscles.

'It doesn't seem fair,' he would complain to the higher-ups, as he puffed and panted beneath his enormous burdens. 'Anyone will tell you I am extremely clever, so why am I never offered a job where I can use my mind?'

And the higher-ups would sneer and tell him to remember his lowly status, and warn him that if he continued to stir up unrest in the colony he would be for it. He was further warned that he was now being watched very closely.

So, in great pain and aware of the many beady eyes upon him, James went about his tasks. But they couldn't stop him thinking, so he thought a lot. He realised that if he had any hope of living to a ripe old age he would have to somehow make it to the top through sheer talent. After much soul-searching he decided to move up a notch by displaying his extraordinary artistic brilliance.

Artists could be found most anywhere in the colony. Often they could be seen painting flattering portraits of the Queen and the higher-ups. While bent double and groaning, James stumbled upon one. The Artist had a far-away look in his eye as he daubed away at a landscape, and a right mess he was making of it too. Hoping to please, James stopped, took up a brush and corrected a few glaring mistakes. The Artist was not pleased at all. In fact he became very angry indeed.

'How dare you turn my landscape into a masterpiece with a few skilful brush-strokes?' he snapped. 'What is the world coming to when common Precious Supply carriers dabble successfully in the Arts? Don't you know your place?'

'I know a lot of things,' admitted James, wincing as his load shifted. 'I was hoping that by showing you how to paint properly you might introduce me into the closed world of the Arts. All I need is a little encouragement...'

'How's this for encouragement?' shouted the Artist. He gave James a savage kick, sending him and his heavy load rolling down the hill. Wagging a warning brush and glaring, the Artist said, 'Hop it, and never come showing me up as a phoney again.'

Deeply humiliated, James staggered away. From that moment on he avoided all sensitive Artists. Instead he set his sights on becoming a Planner. One day, while passing with a double load of Precious Supplies, he came upon one laying out a superb patio for a higher-up he owed a favour to.

'Pardon me,' said James politely, eyeing the Planner's handiwork. 'But if you built the patio so that it blended into the natural lie of the land, it would be more pleasing to the eye, don't you think? If you would permit me to put down my load we could work on it together. Perhaps if you saw my natural talent for planning, you might help me to become a Planner in my own right? If you took advantage of my clever ideas I'm sure the owner would be delighted with the results.'

'What do you mean "delighted"?' said the suspicious Planner. 'Are you accusing me of sucking up to a higher-up by trying to make him happy?'

'Of course not,' hastened James. 'I was merely thinking that if we made a first-class job of the patio, the owner would be pleased, thus making his delight your reward.'

'Now you accuse me of accepting rewards!' shouted the now frightened Planner. 'Well, let me tell you this, accuse me of bribery and corruption in public and I'd drag you through the highest courts in the Colony. I'll give you five seconds to leave with your mouth tight shut, otherwise I will march straight down to the Law Courts and wake up a Judge.'

Miserably, James reeled away, the Planner's threats ringing loud in his ears. He vowed to himself never to excite a touchy Planner again. Anyway, he was beginning to feel that Science was more in his line . . .

The idea became an obsession. As he panted back and forth beneath his heavy loads, he occupied his mind solving the problems of the mysterious Universe. A few days later he had solved most of them, but now he felt too shy about approaching a mad Scientist, and putting him in the picture. Would the Scientists be grateful to hear his exciting new theories, and offer him a job amongst them? Conquering his fears, he approached one. The Scientist was lying on his new patio fast asleep. He was extremely annoyed at being woken up. Through mad eyes he looked James up and down as the proud little ant explained a few Universal mysteries.

'Of course,' James was saying, his words tumbling over each other, 'when I realised that Time was Relative and Space curved back on itself, I was determined to find out the cause. It was when I did some sums in my head and proved that there must be Black Holes in Space, that the truth hit me. That led me to look more closely at Sub-atomic Particles and—'

'You'll be that Precious Supply carrier we have been warned to watch out for,' said the Scientist nastily, interrupting. 'Not content with meddling in the Arts, and offering to plan my patio so as to make it the most superb in the Colony, you now have the cheek to dabble in Science?'

'But just think,' pleaded James. 'If you and me pooled our knowledge we could use our discoveries for the betterment of the whole Colony. Between us we could lighten the burden of the Workers—perhaps even invent a machine that would transfer Precious Supplies from this point to that? Surely you as a responsible Scientist would be happy to see our skills used for peaceful purposes? Alas, I am afraid there are some who would use my theories for destruction. I am thinking of dangerous Sub-atomic Particles getting into the wrong hands . . .'

'What do you mean, "your ideas"?' bristled the Scientist. 'Are you trying to say that I lounge around on this patio just to soak up the sun? Are you suggesting that just because I have my eyes closed all the time, I am fast asleep? And another thing, it just so happens my mind was deep inside a Black Hole when you came along and rudely interrupted my train of thought. As for the Sub-atomic Particle thing, I hope you don't think that I would endanger the Colony by tinkering with something I know nothing about?'

'The thought never crossed my mind,' protested James. 'I am just saying that some Scientists would deliver terrible inventions into the hands of the Military. Now if you would make me your assistant you could rest assured that I would be right behind you to mop up the dangerous mistakes you might make.'

'And who will be toting around your Precious Supplies in the meantime?' sneered the Scientist. 'Anyway, one needs to be an ace at reeling off long columns of meaningless numbers to be a Scientist. The figures don't have to make sense, just impress. I'll give you an example—' And he gabbled off a string of sums that multiplied and subtracted, but added up to nothing. James, a genius at maths, realised that he was being given the brush-off. Deeply shamed, he shouldered his burden and tottered away.

For many weeks he simply went about his thankless work and thought about nothing. Having been snubbed by an Artist, a Planner and a Scientist, his mind was too numb and too hurt to be able to think straight. But as the memory of those painful episodes faded, so he became again aware of all the injustice in the Colony. James realised that the only way to get things put right was to study Law. A few days later he knew everything worth knowing about it. Armed with lots of revolutionary knowledge, he plucked up the courage to approach a Law-maker.

'Excuse me, sir,' he said, shyly accosting one. 'I know I'm only a common Precious Supply carrier, but I was wondering if you could help me to find a junior post in the Law-making process? I feel I am cut out for the job. May I demonstrate my knowledge of your craft? For instance, you will be aware that I am closely watched? Well, sir, I believe this to be wrong. In my few spare moments from drudgery, I worked out a system whereby everyone in the Colony would be free to climb the ladder to the top of the heap without the fear of being marked and watched. I call it

Democracy. I believe that together we could draft some really fair Laws that would sweep away this mockery of a system. For instance, a good new Law would be for everyone in the Colony to pull their full weight. I am thinking about the higher-ups who pile all the work onto the likes of me, and spend too much time lying on their patios. In fact, sir, my dream is for everyone from the highest to the lowest to have a patio. You as a responsible Law-maker will surely see the justice of this?'

'You've been reading my mind,' said the Law-maker smoothly. 'As a matter of fact, I was meaning to bring up those very points at the next Law-making session. It has always been my dearest wish to improve the lot of the Workers. But tell me, don't you agree that before one starts spouting about everyone pulling their weight, one should set an example? Correct me if I'm wrong, but that load you are carrying looks a little light in weight to me. I always thought you lot staggered all over the place beneath a maximum load? Are you aware of the severe penalty I could slap on you for trying to dodge the column?'

'I am not to blame, sir!' cried James, his heart sinking into his aching flat feet. 'I have never dodged a full load in my life. You see, sir, there was a mix-up at the Weighing Station. Being brilliant at sums, I tried to tell the Weighing Authority that they were subtracting instead of adding, but they told me to mind my own business.'

'That's as maybe,' replied the smooth talking Law-maker. 'But if I were you I would nip back to the Weighing Station and make up my quota. Just tell the Authority that they are being closely watched by a powerful Law-maker.'

James, shrewdly guessing that the Law-maker would make it hot for him if he didn't obey, turned to hurry back to the Weighing Station.

'Rest assured,' called the Law-maker after him. 'I will certainly bring up that "patios for all" point at the next session.' With that, he lay back on his own, and was soon snoring.

Then came the day when the Colony declared War on a rival group. The excuse was that the enemy had been holding sneaky War-games in preparation for an attack. The Chief Law-maker stubbornly denied that the home Colony had been doing exactly the same. Thus the jubilant Military came into their own at the top of the heap. For a long time they had been ignored. During the boring Peace they had sprawled about on patios, enviously counting each other's medals, and warning everyone that the Peace couldn't last. Now they were all activity, marching up and down and shouting orders at each other. Because the Military on the other side were doing the same, the dispute became known as The Phoney War, where nothing much happened. The Generals enjoyed this part of the War enormously. They were familiar figures, strutting about at Rear Headquarters, promising the poor conscripted Workers that if they returned from battle they would all have a patio apiece. They had the power to promise this because many of the top Generals were Law-makers, wearing different hats.

Eventually the real War began. The

Workers, hastily crammed into the front line, fell like flies. The dug-outs far to the rear were also full up. These were filled with Generals, all complaining about the Workers who were not winning the War quickly enough, and falling asleep over heavy meals.

As the War dragged on, so the workload of James and his fellow Precious Supply carriers increased. Day and night they tottered to and from the front, near to expiring beneath their burdens. And if that wasn't enough, it was also their duty to carry the fat Generals even farther to the rear when the tide of battle threatened to engulf them. This was because the Generals were so weighed down with medals they couldn't run away fast enough. It was also the job of the carriers to bring back the wounded from the front. This James and his friends gladly did, for not only were the lower orders lighter in weight than the Generals, but they were more likeable.

Yet even amidst the terrible carnage James continued to exercise his brilliant mind. One day he hit upon an idea for ending the War. He also had the perfect opportunity to air it; for, glancing up the stem of a dandelion, he saw a General who had been left behind during a panicky retreat, and had astonishingly managed to shin up it out of harm's way.

'I have been thinking, sir,' said James, craning to address him. 'Instead of trying to knock the enemy for six, why don't we make Peace and vow never to go to War again? After all, sir, does anyone still remember what we are fighting about? And sir, don't you agree that we and the enemy are all brothers under the skin? So if you approve, I could easily draw up a Peace Treaty. I know I'm only a humble Precious Supply carrier, but I think a lot and I am convinced all War is unnecessary and wrong. I am sure that given the chance I could persuade both sides to settle their differences and build a new world based on equality, peace, and prosperity for all.'

'I know you, you cowardly cad!' yelled the General. 'We higher-ups have been warned to watch you closely. Well, let me tell you this, our policy is to continue this War until the enemy is totally wiped out. Who are *you*, a closely watched Precious Supply carrier, to tell me how to lose a War by crawling to the enemy?'

'*End* a War, sir,' replied James, quietly. Groaning softly, he picked up his load and set off for the front once more.

The War ended with both Colonies destroyed. James was amongst the surviving few. This was because he had finally collapsed from exhaustion, the scavenging bands upon the battlefield leaving him for dead. Picking himself up, James sadly surveyed the ruin and wastage spread about him. He returned to the home Colony, quiet and deserted now. Only the Queen remained. But she too was dying, for she no longer had servants to attend her, no one any more to carry the Precious Supplies that were her life-blood. The half-completed highways, the splendid patios, all were fast falling into decay. For a while, James stood gazing in contemplation. Then, suddenly fired with a mission, he left that place and all its unhappy

memories . . .

And so began the Ministry of James. North, south, east and west, from Colony to Colony he preached to small groups of Workers, his voice filled with passion. And the Workers ceased in their toil, put down their burdens to listen.

'One day, together, we will build a perfect society!' he would cry. 'I have a dream that in future times every ant from the highest to the lowest will work for the common good in harmony. And when a satisfying day's work is done, every ant will have his own patio to lounge upon as his right . . .'

His heartfelt and ringing words caused hope to flutter in many a breast. Raptly attentive, the downtrodden masses listened as James preached the Word. But soon a desperate urgency began to fire his soul. Now, at the end of each speech, he would spell out a warning that sent a chill through his listeners. For on his wanderings James's fertile brain had evolved the theory that the Universe had begun with a Big Bang. His dread was that the mad Scientists would absently stumble on this truth and through their meddling bring about the end of the world with another one. For weren't they already tinkering with Sub-atomic Particles as if they were toys?

'Time is fast running out!' James would cry. 'For if the arrogant Scientists refuse to heed my Word, there will be no patios left for anyone to lounge on . . .'

Fearlessly he travelled about the land, not caring that he was being closely watched by the angry Scientists who now ruled the roost at the top of the heap. The germ of an idea became a seed, sown and nurtured by the Ministry of James, and already beginning to blossom into something beautiful and new. But still there were powerful and evil forces, ever eager to crush it. And meanwhile time ticked away . . .

★　　　★　　　★

If, while lounging on your patio, you should see a little ant with a bad back dashing across the paving stones, please, please leave him alone. For he might well be James, the hope of the world . . . Amen.

HAPPY BIRTHDAY, DEAR HOTSPUR

Hotspur was the happiest pig in the farmyard, everyone said so. He was also the most generous, everyone agreed so. In fact Hotspur was one of those pigs who become legends in their own lunchtime. For who else could exist on hardly any food at all, and yet remain so cheerful? Happy, generous, Hotspur was also very very clever. But this was rarely remarked upon, for it was his cheerful kindness that impressed.

'Hotspur is a prince amongst swine,' the others would declare, as he graciously stood back from the swill-tub during mealtimes. 'But loving him as we do, we wish he would take a little more nourishment, he being so painfully thin.'

This was true. Hotspur was a heart-rending sight. He was little more than skin and bone. Yet despite his frailty he managed to remain blissfully content. And he had his hobbies which seemed to give him much satisfaction, to the puzzlement of the other pigs. One hobby was to watch his fellows tucking into their food; the other, racing round and round the farmyard, for Hotspur was a fitness fanatic.

'The mystery deepens,' remarked his friends, between mouthfuls of third helpings. 'Considering Hotspur is fading away to a shadow, his high spirits have us beat.'

But there was really no mystery at all. Being dim and greedy, the other pigs never thought to raise their dripping snouts from the trough, to consider life from all its grim aspects. For food and sleep was their world.

But Hotspur, clever pig, saw the world for what it was. Life was struggle. Or more simply, life was the survival of the thinnest. Yes, Hotspur had good reason to smile. For while the other pigs scoffed away at their hearty meals, he enjoyed an experience they would never know. Birthdays. Hotspur had already celebrated three and was looking forward to his fourth this coming Christmas.

One could always tell when Hotspur's birthday was near. He became nervous and edgy. By the middle of December his bird-like appetite had disappeared completely. In full view of the farmhouse window, he would totter about the yard in a most appealing manner. The hearts of the other pigs would go out to him.

'It will be the excitement,' they agreed, slurping the last dregs from the trough. 'We will probably feel much the same when our own birthdays come around.'

How little they knew.

Then suddenly, one day, holly and a Christmas tree appeared in the farmhouse window. The fat pigs had barely time to comment upon how beautiful the effect was, before being packed into lorries and driven away. But that didn't prevent them from singing, 'Happy birthday, dear Hotspur', before vanishing from view down the long farmhouse drive. After all, Hotspur was their favourite kind of swine.

'Now we wonder where they went?' said the few remaining piglets, in astonishment. And without us, too . . .'

'They have gone on an outing,' explained a happy Hotspur. 'It's a reward for eating up all their swill.'

'So if we eat up all our swill, will we get to go on an outing?' asked the anxious piglets.

'Providing you grow big and fat, you can bet on it,' replied Hotspur. 'Don't fret, for your treat will come next year.'

The small pigs were so pleased to hear this that they sang 'Happy birthday, dear Hotspur' all the way through, and time and time again, until the sun went down. And Hotspur smiled, and thanked them very much.

The months flew by and soon it was autumn again. Apples hung heavy on the boughs, and in the woods the oak trees groaned beneath their burden of acorns. It was a fruitful year indeed.

The piglets, once so small and lean, had become fat and greedy. Hotspur, polite as ever, was still standing aside, inviting the others to tuck into his own portion. Wrinkled and aged he might appear, but he followed his hobbies religiously. Once again he became a

familiar sight as he jogged around the farmyard, determined to sweat off the merest ounce of surplus fat that might threaten his Christmas birthday celebration. And as always he was the agreeable companion, happy, generous and kind.

'Too kind,' agreed the other pigs, shaking their heads as they licked the trough dry. 'But how we wish he would enjoy a good filling meal once in a while.'

For the birthday pig that time was fast approaching.

It was a surprise to everyone. Even Hotspur was taken aback. It appeared that the strange beings who topped up the troughs with swill, and put holly in the window at Christmas time, had noted the glut of acorns, and had decided to take advantage of this unexpected windfall. After all, the price of swill being what it was these days. For the next few weeks, acorns by the sackful were tipped into the pig compound.

Thinking that he was an expert on autumns, having experienced four, the other pigs questioned Hotspur about this strange turn of events. He could give no answer, for he was as mystified as they. The supply seemed unlimited. The pigs agreed that acorns were quite tasty. Hotspur, cautiously nibbling one, thought them to be the food of the Gods. He soon became severely addicted. Gone for ever was the kindly and cheerful Hotspur of old. He became mean and dangerous, constantly accusing the other pigs of stealing his share. They denied this.

'Have them all, if you wish,' they said generously. 'We prefer swill anyway. Acorns are a little too bland for our taste. Now it is our turn to be kind, for we have sponged on you for long enough.'

As autumn lengthened into winter the amount of acorns Hotspur put away was extraordinary. The other pigs watched in awe as he chomped away, warily keeping their distance, for his eyes were ever meanly alert for thieves who might steal his treasure. No longer did he take his morning and evening jogs around the farmyard. Indeed, the only exercise he took these days was when he would rear up against the fence of the compound, grunting soulfully to indicate that his supply of acorns was running low. But soon even this became impossible. Enormously fat now, he could only lie on his side and squeal with pleasure as yet more sackfuls of bounty were tipped over the fence . . .

Then one frosty day there appeared in the farmyard window some sprigs of holly and a Christmas tree. Too late did Hotspur realise that his fourth birthday was on top of him. Then the lorries arrived. In vain did Hotspur suck in his cheeks to appear thin and wasted. He was the first to be hoisted aboard, hoisted because his legs were unable to bear his enormous weight. As the lorries rumbled away down the long drive, the few remaining pigs did not forget to congratulate their departing friend. A once happy swine raised his head to listen to the strains of an old and familiar tune, getting fainter and fainter as he was borne away . . .

'. . . Happy birthday, dear Hotspur, Happy birthday to you . . .'

ALL WAS WELL
IN THE WOOD

It had been a long hard winter, biting deep into the year. At last it was over. Spring flowers bloomed and quickly faded, summer stock was soon knee-high and gaining. Homes were fast vanishing behind fresh green leaf. Nature was hurrying, catching up. Now the pace slackened as balance was restored. All was in time and place. All was well in the wood ... or was it ... ?

High above in the fork of an elm a battle raged. It was fought in silence and the outcome seemed certain. There would be no witness to mourn the defeated. But soon, many would hear the cry of triumph ringing through the wood.

The chick had attacked at first light. His tactic was surprise. Before long there was no doubt as to which way the battle was going. The chick fought confidently, as if he knew right to be on his side. Twice he had his victim teetering over the edge of the nest. The next attempt would surely succeed. Tired but jubilant, he rested, eyeing his panting rival with hatred.

The other chick was quite bewildered. Time and again he had fought to resist the cowardly attacks. Although the first-born and larger of the two, he had been caught off-balance, and was paying the price. But he was desperate to live. He knew his survival depended on the next and final round. Should he himself go over to the attack, and at least go down fighting? But though the idea was sound he lacked the will, his heart wasn't in it. All he wished for was to be left alone.

Alone ... now, that struck a chord. Instinct nudged at his confused mind. Then he had no more time to think, for his opponent was shaping up for the last bout. One couldn't help but admire the attacker. He didn't look the warrior type at all. It was hard to believe that only hours ago he had been snug inside his shell. But the evidence was there. Scraps of blue shell still clung to his downy face.

His body, with its few stubby feathers, looked pathetically fragile. But his lust for battle was alarming. Fragile or not, he seemed determined to toss the other, larger chick, to a certain death below. He prepared to charge.

Suddenly at that moment, all became clear to the larger chick. The thoughts that had nagged away at the back of his mind surged forward to transform him. He felt a deep anger. Why was he allowing the other to push him about so? Where was his own drive and dash, for hadn't nature designed him for precisely this situation? He realised now that if he lost this battle, it could signal the beginning of the end for his kind. Not only his life, but the survival of his species was at stake in this final clash. Even as the enemy charged he knew exactly his role in this affair. Smoothly, efficiently, he swung into action. An inborn and pitiless cunning ended the battle right there. Nimbly sidestepping, he watched without emotion as his small rival plunged fluttering to the forest floor.

Alone and victorious, he savoured the

morning air, stretching his legs, and flexing stubby wings. He felt ravenously hungry. He knew that quite soon breakfast would arrive. But today there would be no jealous fighting for shares. He would enjoy this meal alone as he would every other. He would grow strong, his future assured, now that the competition had been eliminated. Strong, in order to deal swiftly with his remaining enemy, for he had murderous plans for the single blue egg that still shared the nest with him. He felt neither malice nor regret as he stared at that warm, already tap-tapping oval. He simply knew that this was the way things should be.

The black speck in the clear blue sky came nearer. Soon the air became disturbed as the provider hovered over the nest. A great joy swelled the breast of the young bird. Clambering onto the side of the nest he gave vent to his feelings. He lived, the world should know it. His cry was harsh and ill-formed. But another, far away over the wood, heard it, and also rejoiced. His real parent, content with a plan

successfully realised, sang loud and clear
. . . 'cuckoo, cuckoo, cuckoo . . .'
All was well in the wood.

THE END OF THE TALE

'Are you really as old as the world itself?' asked the small creatures of the Plain.

The Great Yellow-tailed Snake seemed not to hear. He continued to stare at the eastern horizon. Each day from dawn till dusk he gazed so, his eyes always hopeful.

'And is it true that while your nose rests here in Africa, the end of your tail lives across the ocean? A little bird told us so.'

The great snake sighed and shifted, the movement causing a minor earthquake two continents away.

'They say you are the unhappiest snake in the world. Why so, for isn't life the greatest treasure of all...?'

'And you with so much of it to spare,' said the envious.

Kindly though he was, the snake did not reply. He had been asked those same questions so many times down through the centuries. Instead he smiled his sad smile and tried to enjoy the warmth of the sun setting over his midriff, far, far to the west.

'Are you unhappy because you have a dream that will never come true?' the small ones persisted. 'That is often the reason for sadness like yours.'

The Great Yellow-tailed Snake nodded gently, then closed his eyes as if to sleep awhile.

The small creatures of the Plain were not afraid of the giant in their midst. Often during the hours of hot sunshine they would lie in his shade. At night-time many snuggled close to his scaly bulk, fearing the fierce cats that stalked the darkness. Birds built their nests in the thick creeper that draped his sides. He had long been a landmark for the herds of migrating deer, yearly following his winding contours to the rich grazing lands. He was as familiar and enduring as the snow-capped mountains. Lakes and valleys had yet to be formed when the great snake was already ancient. Of all the wonders of the world he was the most awesome. And because of his age-long sadness, the loneliest.

Born back in the mists of time, in

mere days he had freakishly outgrown the largest of his kind. A century later his tail was miles away, cutting a deep swathe through the western rain forests. And as his kinsmen lived and died he alone endured, ever growing, always gazing hopefully towards the eastern horizon.

The sun finally set. The small creatures of the Plain no longer played, no longer asked their questions. For them it was time to face the serious business of surviving through the night. Life for them was short, and therefore to be protected and treasured. As the moon rose many were tucked away in the shielding comfort of their great friend, dreaming that they too were as old as the world itself, with centuries before them. For how they envied the Great Yellow-tailed Snake. How unfair, they grieved, that time had not likewise befriended them. But they would never know the sadness locked away in the great snake's heart. How could they have known that he in turn envied them?

That night, unsleeping, the great snake gazed at the stars. They were the companions of his loneliness, each a friend. A million times he had whispered of his misery and hopes across the vastness of space. And as they twinkled it seemed that they understood and sympathised. For they too were victims of all that dreary time behind and before. For the gift mere mortals desired soon staled. As the great snake watched, the stars gathered spent comets, and waited for the end their birth had signalled.

Centuries, many thousands, slowly passed. Then came a time when the sun grew hot and swollen, its daily climb across the sky sluggish now. And the earth, wreathed in mists, began to dribble out its few remaining days. Now the heavens were crammed with dying stars, each streaking for the pin-point in space they would all seek to occupy.

Fate, as if at last recognising the misery of the Great Yellow-tailed Snake, dealt him a kindness. Across the hot and barren Plain came crawling a small one of his kind. Cold, alone and afraid, the youngster huddled against the huge nose of his ancient kinsman. And he was gladly welcomed, for the great snake had been without company for far too long. He was quite blind now, his eyes burned out centuries ago by the searing sun. But still those unseeing sockets faced eastwards, for habit was a long time dying.

Sensing the small snake's fear, the great one sought to comfort him in the only way he knew. He told him a story. The tale began with his birth all that incredible time ago. He described the beauty of a once-youthful earth with its teeming life. He told of the rise and fall of mountains, and of the many species who had fought to survive, only to become extinct in a mere morning of his own lifetime. And how, down the ages, he alone had endured, ever growing, and ever the lonelier as all dwindled to dust about him ... At this point his story stopped as grief overwhelmed him. He seemed unable to speak further. It was as if he was suffering from some inner torment that he could not trust himself to speak of.

But the little snake was shrewd, despite his lack of worldliness. He had

listened intently throughout. And without being told, he sensed instinctively the old blind one's longings. For wasn't he himself a Yellow-tailed Snake? For a long time he gazed into the sightless eyes of the other, his own kind little heart sharing the pain as only another Yellow-tailed Snake could. And as he imagined and shared that dreadful anguish, so he gently chewed the end of his tail, the action being both natural and comforting. For Yellow-tailed Snakes were like that. How could one possibly cope with and enjoy life, without the end of one's tail to chew upon? The little snake continued to gaze pityingly at the saddened giant. No wonder the other had never dared speak of his heartache. For what self-respecting snake of their kind would admit that the end of one's tail was dearer than life itself, and thus invite ridicule? So instead, the great snake had chosen to suffer in silence down through all those ages. Hope alone had kept him going. Hope that perhaps one day . . .

The small snake turned his head westwards, noting how the bulk of his

kinsman wound and twisted over the angrily steaming landscape, before disappearing from view over the horizon. He began to think aloud ...'
'And did he not say that the earth is round? So that is what he waits for ...' Excitedly, expectantly, the youngster turned about again. As dawn began to break so the sighted and the blind stared eastwards. Slowly a dull yellow glow appeared above the distant hills. As the awe-struck little snake watched, so his heart leapt with joy. For that round glow seemed to be advancing towards them across the Plain ...

The old snake felt the familiar heat of sunrise upon his face. But somehow this morning it was different. The usual pleasing warmth seared like a furnace. Distantly, above the sudden roar of earthquake, he could hear the excited voice of the young snake—the voice of one who looked through eyes seeing all they would ever see.

'Old one!' he cried. 'That I should be born at such a time. Your unhappiness is over. Let me be your eyes, for here is the end of your tail!'

Amidst the crash and rumble of a dying earth ended a tale. And incidentally, the full circle of another. Together, beneath a myriad stars colliding at that pin-point in space, patiently waited two Great Yellow-tailed Snakes, each with a tail tucked comfortingly in his mouth . . .

Photoset, printed and bound in Great Britain by
REDWOOD BURN LIMITED, Trowbridge, Wiltshire